Stepping Out

Laura Langston

O F   S

Library and Archives Canada Cataloguing in Publication

Langston, Laura, 1958-, author
Stepping out / Laura Langston.
(Orca limelights)

Issued in print and electronic formats.
ISBN 978-1-4598-0895-9 (paperback).—ISBN 978-1-4598-0896-6 (pdf).—
ISBN 978-1-4598-0897-3 (epub)

I. Title. II. Series: Orca limelights
PS8573.A5832S74 2016   jc813'.54   C2015-904484-7
                                             C2015-904485-5

First published in the United States, 2016
Library of Congress Control Number: 2015946396

Summary: Paige Larsson, YouTube comedy vlogger, has always used humor
to cope with her disability—but an opportunity to compete in stand-up
comedy is a big step out of her comfort zone in this novel for teens.

*Orca Book Publishers is dedicated to preserving the environment and has printed
this book on Forest Stewardship Council® certified paper.*

Orca Book Publishers gratefully acknowledges the support for
its publishing programs provided by the following agencies:
the Government of Canada through the Canada Book Fund and the
Canada Council for the Arts, and the Province of British Columbia
through the BC Arts Council and the Book Publishing Tax Credit.

Cover design by Rachel Page
Cover photography by Getty Images

ORCA BOOK PUBLISHERS
www.orcabook.com

Printed and bound in Canada.

19 18 17 16 • 4 3 2 1

For Zachary, because he always makes me laugh

One

*ast Paige Friday: I am so over mushrooms.
Hello, people? Mushrooms are a fungus!
They breed in warm, wet, smelly places and
they spread. How do I know this? My sister started
growing mushrooms in her warm, wet, smelly room
last week, and this morning when I was in the
bathroom I saw her newest eye shadow. It's called*
Portobello Pewter. *Well, I have some suggestions
for my sister. How about* Shiitake Spice *lipstick?
Or* Oyster Bomb *blush? She could even make her
own conditioner—*Cremini Crème Ultimate Control.
I did, and look how well it turned out for me.

"It's not *Portobello Pewter*, it's *Passionate Pewter*,
and you had no right to tell people what's in my

makeup bag!" my sister says when I walk into the school bathroom Friday at lunch.

My stomach sinks. Even though my latest video has already gotten twenty thousand views—*twenty thousand!*—I don't need this. Not now. I'm in a hurry, and my sister, Brooke, is the last person I want to see. She's at the counter by the window, shaping her nails with a fuchsia file and looking bored as always. Even her hair (blond, long, perfect) looks bored. Her two best friends are with her. Twin One is inspecting her eyebrows in the bathroom mirror. Twin Two is surfing on her phone. Brooke points her nail file at me. Sunlight glints off the tip. It looks like a magic witch wand. "You've crossed a line this time, Paige."

As far as my sister is concerned, I've crossed a line with every single YouTube video I've uploaded in the last nine months. "I didn't look in your makeup bag," I say.

I didn't have to. Brooke spreads her makeup all over the bathroom counter. It's impossible to miss.

"What I do in my room is my business," she says.

That's why I didn't film the piece in her room. I filmed it in the bathroom, balancing my new camera on the vanity shelf. Okay, so I did use her blush and lipstick to illustrate a point. With a mushroom or two. Hey, props matter.

"You shouldn't have told people I'm growing mushrooms." She glares at me. "You know what Mom says. Home stuff stays at home. It's private."

The only part of private I'm interested in right now is privacy to use the toilet. I don't have time for yet another argument with my sister. I don't need any hassles from Twin One or Twin Two either. Not with Carly waiting for me in the cafeteria. I can't wait to tell her my news. In two hours, I've gotten the most views I've ever had on a single video. And last night I reached five thousand subscribers! I'm on a roll. "Oh, excuse me. I didn't know the mushroom-growing operation for *your science class* was covert."

The twins snicker. Brooke shoots them a look. Twin One smothers her giggle with a cough. Twin Two hides behind her cell phone. I walk with as much grace as I can to the stall. Should I leave without washing my hands when I'm done? The last thing I need is more grief from my sister.

I'm still considering my options when I finish and exit the stall. Brooke stares at me. "That was seriously the lamest piece of Internet I've seen in months," she says. My insides turn to water. "Totally *lame*-o-rama," she repeats.

My breath catches in my throat, but I don't flinch. I don't even blink. I gaze back at her, my face carefully blank. There is a challenge in her hazel eyes, and I've never been one to back down from a challenge. Especially not one from my sister. At least, that's what I tell myself as I make my way to the sink. The truth is slightly more complicated. One, I'm a bit of a germophobe. I mean, come on. We are talking school bathroom. Two, I only pretend to be brave. Fake it till you make it and all that.

"Thanks for watching." I squirt pink soap into my palm. "I can use all the views I can get." I'm determined to be the youngest comedy star in the history of YouTube. As big as Jenna Marbles or Grace Helbig. Why go to college when you can make people laugh for a living?

"Who said I watched it?" Brooke says.

"Obviously you watched it." I lather up. "Otherwise, how would you know it was lame?"

She rolls her eyes. Twin One and Twin Two shake their heads. Clearly they don't have my sister's eye-rolling skills.

Brooke has been seriously pissed at me since this started last fall. I did a stand-up routine in drama class and was so stoked with the way it turned out that I created a YouTube channel—PrecisePaige—and recorded and uploaded the routine. Being on YouTube was such a rush, I kept going. I did a few more, focusing on comedy over special effects and using the webcam on my laptop. They were basic but rough, especially in the first few months. After a while, though, I learned about lighting and props and editing, and I decided my laptop wouldn't cut it for shooting outside the house. So I upgraded my old camera, bought some software and began creating and uploading funny vlogs three times a week. I called them *First Paige Monday, Paige Notes Wednesday* and *Last Paige Friday.* And now, nine months later, I'm starting to get a YouTube following.

"People talk," my sister says as I rinse my hands.

She's right. And thank God for that. First it was the kids at school. Then, when I did one about my parents being into porcelain (mom is a dentist and dad is a plumber), my grandpa started watching. Grandpa was horrified, because I did it sitting on this old pink toilet Dad stores in the basement.

I don't know why he freaked. I kept my clothes on. I even found some pink dental molds to use as props. Anyway, he told his friends at his retirement villa, who told their friends, and, well, the views started climbing and the comments kept coming. Now I actually have fans. Me, Paige Larsson of Bellevue, Washington. And last month, one of the free Seattle entertainment papers even wrote me up for its *Teens to Watch* column.

Brooke hates that I'm getting all this attention. She never misses a chance to tell me how terrible I am. In fact, she sometimes texts me right after I upload, though today she has spared me that fate. Instead, she has used the word *lame* to describe my latest offering. That word has been off-limits since grade four, and she knows it.

She sniffs. "I don't have to watch it to know."

Brooke will always be ahead of me. She is ten months older than I am and a whole lot prettier. But like the rest of the human race, she is flawed. And one of her flaws is a lack of common sense.

"True." I reach for a paper towel. "The phrase 'the lamest piece of Internet I've *seen in months*' could be interpreted in so many ways."

A burst of color flares on her cheeks.

"Maybe you only imagined you saw it and imagined that I was terrible, and you were using a figure of speech." I give her my biggest smile. "Because we both know that was a pretty awesome *Last Paige Friday* I did."

Her eyes flash. "No, it wasn't."

"Perhaps you perceived my performance psychically or discerned it on a dust mote by osmosis. Or maybe you had a reliable friend tell you all the funky fungal details." A teeny grin from Twin Two.

"Give it up, Paige. Nobody thinks you're funny." Brooke tosses her bag over her shoulder.

"Or maybe," I say slyly, "it was the altered state you were in."

A tiny frown puckers her brow. My sister not only lacks common sense, she's a little slow sometimes too.

"From the mushrooms?" I prompt.

"Oh my god." With a snort of disgust, she pushes away from the counter.

I smirk. "Eating hallucinogens will do it to you every time."

The bathroom door flies open, banging against the wall. We all jump. Our vice-principal,

Ms. Vastag, marches into the room. She's a short, stout woman with an overbite and long gray hair she wears in a braid. "Who's eating hallucinogens?" She studies the four of us. "You know we have zero tolerance for drugs in this school."

Ms. Vastag is known for her potty mouth and her purple Birkenstocks. She wears them year-round, rain, snow or sun. Today she's paired them with men's work socks, a denim skirt that's obscenely tight across her ample stomach and a red sweatshirt stained with whatever they were eating in her foods class last block.

"We know," I say. I don't need to look at Brooke to sense her fear. She's been caught smoking a couple of times this year, and last month she and Twin Two were caught with beer out on the soccer field. One more mess-up, and she won't be allowed to attend grad.

Ms. Vastag holds out her hand. "Hand it over—and no fooling around, because I'll search all four of you if I have to."

"We don't have anything," Brooke says in a tiny voice. "Really." The twins exchange furtive looks. No doubt one of them has a pack of cigarettes. Not a big deal, but Lampshire Heights takes a hard line on cigarettes, alcohol and anything similar on school property.

Ms. Vastag's eyes narrow. "How about we continue this conversation in my office then?"

"There's no need for that." I sigh, like this whole mess is my fault. Which it kind of is. I pull out a piece of dried-up brown mushroom left over from this morning's YouTube video. "This is it," I say. "Though we didn't get around to eating it yet."

Ms. Vastag peers at my hand. "That's not a hallucinogen. That's a cremini. At least, I think it is." She looks up at me. "Are you having me on, Larsson?"

I keep my mouth shut and shrug.

She waves her hand at Brooke and the twins. "You three can go." They scurry out the door like rats racing for cover. She turns back to me. "What's the story here? Be serious for once in your life."

My flaw is that I generally speak before thinking, and I usually say whatever's on my mind too. Sometimes this leads to problems. Like now. Having already started down the hallucinogen road, I'm not sure how to get out of it unless I admit to being stupid. Since that's the truth (and since I'm desperate to get out of the bathroom and go see Carly), I decide it's the best choice. "I was bugging my sister," I say. "That's all."

Ms. Vastag studies me for a minute. Then she sighs. "That is not the kind of thing I like to see my students joking about. Meet me in my office in five."

Oh *crap.*

She stomps out the door.

I stand on my toes, take aim and pitch my soiled paper towel directly into the garbage can.

Slam dunk.

I should be thinking about Ms. Vastag and the mess I've made. But I'm not. *Nobody thinks you're funny.* My mind hums with the insult. *Totally lame.* I feel myself slip-sliding into that black pit of self-hate that started in elementary school. Refusing to go there, I quickly yank my thoughts back. Totally lame? Yeah, okay, maybe. But today—this very minute—twenty thousand people think I'm funny. I grin. Brooke is wrong.

Slam dunk two.

Two

"**I** can't believe Vastag insisted on getting a mushroom-identifying book from the bio lab to confirm that your mushroom really was a cremini," Carly says twenty minutes later as I eat a burger and fries in the cafeteria. "And then lectured you for another five minutes about how inappropriate it is to joke about taking drugs."

I know. She was so harsh it was like I *was* carrying a magic mushroom in my pocket instead of a dried-out cooking one.

"She should know never to take you seriously," Carly adds.

A burst of laughter interrupts her rant. We're sitting near the front of the cafeteria, just a few tables away from the order counter and one table over from a group of noisy jocks.

I'm not surprised Carly picked the table. She's crushing on one of the basketball players. If I'd gotten here first, I would have headed for a quieter spot in the corner.

"Forget that! Didn't you hear what I said about my latest video? It's already gotten 20,069 views, and it's only been up two and a half hours." I swirl a fry through my pool of ketchup. "I bet I hit 30,000 by the end of the day. It's unreal!"

Carly spoons some peach yogurt out of her cup and says something, but I can't make out her words. I frown and shake my head. When she leans across the table, her dark hair dangles into her yogurt. "When are you going to start monetizing?" she shouts into my ear.

Monetizing. Letting Google upload ads to my videos so I can start making money. "Not quite yet," I shout back, lifting the hair out of her lunch. I love comedy. I do. To me, it's not just light entertainment or a way to kill time. To me, laughter is as important as breath. It takes the sting out of life's crap. It eases the pain of nasty comments and dirty looks. It helps me get through agonizing moments in gym class and awkward pauses at parties. Yes, I want a career in it.

I *will* have a career in it. But I'm only fifteen. I have a few more years until my best-before date expires.

"You need to be more aggressive," Carly says.

Aggressive is Carly's middle name. My middle name is *Naptime.* "I'll get to it." It's not an easy moneymaker, especially with YouTube constantly changing the earning rules. One way or another, though, to make any money you need lots of subscribers. I should have ten thousand by next September. I've told Carly I'll start looking at the business stuff then.

Entire careers have been made in YouTube comedy. Tyler Oakley and Jenna Marbles started there, and they're huge stars now. Mega rich too. And money is good. It'll show my parents that a career in comedy isn't a waste of time. Plus it'll help me avoid Dumpster diving for food when I move away from home.

The jocks get up to leave. The noise level around us drops to a semi-normal state. As I push my half-finished plate of fries over to Carly, my cell phone signals a text. I wipe the grease from my fingers and dig it out of my pants pocket.

Where R U?

Hunter. My heart goes squidgy. He's texted me with the same question three times in the last five minutes, but it's been so loud I haven't heard my phone. "It's Hunter," I tell Carly. But she's staring at the basketball player and doesn't respond.

Eating in the caf, I text back. **Front and center by the food line.**

B right there.

"He's coming over."

Carly turns back to me. "What?" There's a distant, dreamy look in her blue eyes. "Who?"

"Hunter."

"Ooooh." She gives me a knowing smile.

Heat hits the back of my neck. "Shut up and eat a fry."

"Have you told him?"

I sip my chocolate milk and don't say anything. Carly has this crazy idea that I should tell Hunter exactly how I feel. Which is totally ridiculous. Guys don't tell girls how they feel. Well, okay, technically they do, but only in the *you make me want to explode* kind of way, and that's more about biology than any heart-to-heart thing.

"I take it that's a no," she says.

"Have you told basketball guy how you feel?" I ask.

"I barely know him." She reaches for a fry. "We don't share history the way you and Hunter do."

It's true. I've known Hunter MacRae since grade two. Back then, he was the one who kindly explained that the other kids weren't laughing at the fact that my skirt was accidentally stuck in my underpants after I went to the bathroom, they were laughing because my purple-and-orange Halloween underpants were really funny. *I* was really funny, he told me. And people really, really liked funny girls.

A part of me fell in love with comedy that day. The other part fell hard for Hunter MacRae. It was all good until a year or so ago. We lived on the same street; we walked to school together. I supported him through his parents' divorce. He supported me through the pain of being bossed around by Brooke. But things changed at the start of grade ten. My friendly feelings toward him became much, much friendlier. The girl equivalent of *you make me want to explode.* Hunter does not, I guarantee, feel the same way about me.

"You need to get over yourself and tell him," Carly says.

"We're friends. I'm not going to take a chance and spoil that." It's a conversation Carly and I have had so often in the last few months, I can practically recite the lines in my sleep. "Besides, Hunter doesn't like redheads. He likes brunettes." In fact, last year I was pretty sure Hunter and Carly were going to hook up. I'll bet Hunter would go for it. But Carly likes the athletic types, and Hunter's only declared sport to date is potato-chip eating. (His record is fourteen bags of Salt & Pepper chips in one twenty-four-hour period.)

"It's not about the hair, Paige." She dabs her lips with a napkin.

That's easy for her to say. Carly has long dark Kate Middleton hair. Mine is the female equivalent of Prince Harry's: red and frizzy, especially in the rain. And in Seattle, it's either raining or about to rain.

"It's not about your limp either."

I almost choke on a fry. I can't believe she's said it. I glance around to see if anybody's heard her, but nobody's paying attention. "I never said it was," I finally manage.

16

She levels me with a look. "No, but you've thought it."

Carly knows me almost as well as Hunter does. We've been friends since elementary school too. "Don't look for a job working the psychic hotline," I tell her. "Your mind-reading skills suck." We both know I am lying.

When we were younger, I had a name for my gimpy leg. I called it Fred (as long as Brooke wasn't around to make fun). We talked about Fred sometimes like he was a poor, needy relative that I had to endure. I can't remember when that whole thing stopped, but it petered out—or maybe I should say it Fredded out—somewhere in middle school, when the whole pairing-off thing started up. I became painfully aware that guys didn't date girls like me. They hung out with them, they accepted homework answers from them, and on good days they laughed with them. That was enough.

I catch sight of a familiar face. Hunter. My heart squidges in triple time. At least, it used to be enough. But now, as I watch him walk toward us, I'm not so sure. "Don't you dare say anything," I hiss to Carly.

She picks up her juice box. "You know I won't."

And I do know, because Carly has never betrayed me. I can trust her.

"Hey!" he says when he reaches us.

"Hey," I say back. Hunter's face is a little on the longish side, and his brows could use some manscaping, but he has the best voice in the world. Smooth and deep and hot, like espresso loaded with sugar. I swear he could make a ton of money with that voice. His jeans brush against my leg as he slides into the seat beside me. Heat races into my cheeks. Plus, he has an amazing body. And perfectly straight, überwhite teeth (this counts—yes, I am my mother's daughter).

"I saw your latest video." He helps himself to a fry. "Great job!"

Hunter has been my biggest fan since grade two. That, at least, hasn't changed. "Thanks." I push the other half of my burger toward him. He picks it up. Three bites later, it's gone. He wipes his fingers and pulls a piece of paper from his jeans.

"Look." He lays it on the table and smooths it with the palm of his hand.

I glimpse a picture of some teens and bright-blue lettering above them. *The International Te—*

Carly snatches the paper up before I can finish reading. "Are these the details?" she asks him.

"Yeah."

"Cool." She starts to read.

"What details?" I ask.

Carly looks at Hunter. Hunter looks at me, though not exactly at me—more at my nose. And then he clears his throat.

My spine tingles. Hunter only clears his throat when he's nervous. Or mad.

"What?" I ask a second time.

"It's the International Teens in Comedy Festival," he says. "It's happening in Portland a few weeks from now."

Everybody knows about the International Teens in Comedy Festival. At least, anybody interested in comedy. It's huge.

"And you're going," Hunter says.

I laugh. "Sure I am." You don't just *go* to the ITCF. First you have to be nominated. Then you have to go through a rigorous deal to get on the shortlist. Only the best go to the finals. "Come on, guys, that's the Super Bowl of comedy. Get serious."

"I *am* serious," Hunter says.

My left eye starts to twitch.

Carly pushes the paper across the table toward me. "We submitted three of your YouTube vlogs as part of the nomination process," she says. "You've aced the first round of eliminations. You've been shortlisted."

Three

arly has to be kidding. My eye twitch spreads to my cheek. Isn't this the first sign of a stroke? My two best friends are trying to kill me. "No way," I manage.

"Yes, way." Hunter smiles. "They have your email. They'll be sending you the official letter soon."

Blood thumps in my ears. This is crazy. Insane. Like some kind of wacky dream. Or nightmare. I'm not sure which. "I got *shortlisted* for the ITCF?"

"I *know*! Isn't it unreal?" Carly's voice is one decibel below a screech. "You've been working so hard and doing all these amazing videos, and you're finally getting the recognition you deserve."

I *have* been working hard. Doing the vlogs.
Networking with other YouTubers. Comedy is
what I want to do with my life. Making people
laugh comes as easily to me as breathing.
Although right now the breathing part is a
problem, since I feel like I have an elephant on
my chest. Me, *shortlisted.*

I crash back to earth. "I can't go to Portland."

"What?" Carly frowns. "Why? You're banned
from the city? Allergic to the air down there?
What's the deal?"

"That's stand-up," I tell them. "You know I
don't do that." I love the *idea* of stand-up. I do.
It's a thrill hearing somebody laugh at something I say, especially if I'm in drama class or
hanging out with friends. It's my kind of high.
Most people drink when they're at parties.
I make people laugh. It's a total win-win: no
hangover for me and lots of laughs for everybody else. But being in drama class or at a
party with people who've known me since...
well...the purple-and-orange panty days is way
different than being onstage in front of a bunch
of strangers.

Strangers who may not find me funny at all.

"They have a new category this year," Carly says. "For online comedy." She taps the paper in front of me. "Look."

I start to read. *The International Teens in Comedy Festival is pleased to announce a new category this year—video comedy. We're looking for the mega stars of the future in this growing area of performance art. To qualify, interested participants must submit three videos for consideration by February 28.*

I look up. "I can't believe you gave them my contact information. And submitted three of my vlogs without even telling me."

Carly grins like she's won the lottery. "Would you have submitted them?"

"No."

"My point exactly."

"Keep reading," Hunter says.

I look back down. *Those who make the shortlist must travel to Portland for the final elimination rounds. At that time, they must be prepared to submit two previously unseen comedy videos, and they must compete with other shortlisted video contestants and do a series of stand-up routines in front of a live audience.*

I suck in a breath. A live audience? Walking across a stage? No way. "I can't do that."

"Yes, you can," Carly says. "We've talked about this, Paige. You can't hide in your room forever. If you're going to have the comedy career you want, you need to demonstrate range. You need to be way more versatile."

As far as Carly's concerned, I should charge after everything I want in life. A career in comedy. Hunter. Straight hair. "I'm working on it," I tell her. "Look at all the vlogs I've done. On everything from how to kiss a guy with facial hair to dating a toaster. And it's not like I just sit there and talk into the camera either. I *do* stuff. How about that one where I demonstrated fifty uses for popcorn? And don't forget my driving video."

Until today, that was my most popular video ever. I did it from my car, on ways to fake out your driving instructor. I got five hundred subscribers in two days with that one. Two weeks later I also got a nasty letter from an uptight guy at the Washington State Department of Licensing, but I didn't care because (a) I'd gotten my license the week before and (b) you haven't arrived until you start getting hate mail.

"You need to learn other forms of comedy. Like improv and stand-up," she says.

I've been *shortlisted* for the ITCF.

"Stand-up is dying," I tell her. I've been shortlisted for the ITCF. Me. Paige Larsson. As I try to process my conflicting emotions (joy/horror/elation/panic), I do what I always do: speak my mind. "Who wants to get all dressed up and go sit in a cold, noisy club somewhere? My grandpa, that's who. And pretty soon all those old people will die off and everybody else will be sitting at home in their pajamas, laughing at YouTube. YouTube is a community. I can interact with people. Comment on other videos. Get to know my fans. And I can make money too. YouTube is perfect."

"It's perfect *today*," Carly corrects. "But what's coming next month? Next year? You've got five thousand subscribers. You've had twenty thousand views to date. That's not enough."

I know she's right. On the other hand, I have been picking up close to six hundred subscribers a month. And that's pretty good, considering I only upload a few times a week. It's not like this is my full-time job. Yet.

"We've been studying this in my social media class," she continues. "People like Oakley and Marbles are getting numbers into the millions."

I'd love that, but it takes years of work to get those kinds of numbers. And I've got school to think about. My part-time job at the pool. I tune Carly out. Go to Portland? Get up onstage in front of a bunch of strangers? Could I? It's the kind of thing I've always dreamed of. But in my dreams I glide out effortlessly, graceful and sure. I don't limp across the stage with a twisted foot. Or frizzy red hair. I glance at Hunter. He's staring at his knuckle like it holds the answer to all of life's mysteries. Finally he looks at Carly.

"Why don't you quit talking," he says, "and let her read the rest of it."

Hunter's middle name is *To the Point*. I start reading again.

Winners will receive $10,000 for themselves and $10,000 for their school drama or video department. Ten grand? Whoa! *They will also receive a one-year contract with the Endless Field Agency and a one-month intensive with Kids Zone Comedy Troupe in New York.* Oh my god. I feel like all the air has been punched out of my chest. I gasp in a breath.

Endless Field represents Ellen DeGeneres and Amy Poehler. They handle social media platforming, sponsorships, agent representation. And Kids Zone Comedy is known for turning teen comic wannabes into stars.

Winners must be available to travel to New York City at least once during the twelve months following the win. Judging for this category will be led by Raven Prest.

Travel to New York. Raven Prest!

It's a good thing I'm sitting down, because I am so light-headed I swear I could pass out. I love Raven Prest. She's up there with Sarah Silverman and Jenna Marbles. She started out on YouTube, but she has her own comedy show now. Rumor has it she'll be hosting the Academy Awards next year. "I can't afford to pass this up." My voice comes out in a barely-there whisper. It's the truth, and it's probably the hardest thing I've ever said.

"Of course you can't." Carly rolls her eyes. "What do you think we've been telling you!"

My friends—my best friends in the entire world—have landed me the biggest opportunity ever. And I am terrified beyond belief. Grandpa has a saying: *Life is either preparation for success or preparation for failure.* Well, here it is. My opportunity for success. Except...what if I fail?

"But Portland?" I say. For once I'm not saying all of what I'm thinking. *That means I'll have to limp across the stage in front of a bunch of strangers.* "I can't take time off school. I don't have money for a hotel. My parents will never let me drive the van down to Oregon." They don't even like me taking I-5 into town.

Carly starts to speak, but Hunter holds up his hand. "The competition is on the weekend, so you wouldn't miss school. Two nights' hotel is covered for the finalists. And you don't need to worry about driving to Portland. That's taken care of."

"What are you talking about?"

Carly chews the corner of her lip. "Don't freak," she says.

Nerves flutter in my stomach. As if I could freak out any more than I already am. "What?"

Hunter clears his throat. My spine tingles a second time. What aren't they telling me? I stare at him. His blue eyes can't quite meet mine. "A pile of us are going to Portland with you."

I snicker. "Yeah right, sure you are."

Hunter pulls out his phone and taps the screen. Five seconds later, the school website appears. He shoves it under my nose. "Look."

There it is, front and center under the big black Lampshire Heights logo. *See Paige Win. Congratulations, Paige Larsson, on being short-listed for the International Teens in Comedy Festival. Join us April 3 when a group of us will travel down to Portland to see Paige win.*

I am so stunned my mouth refuses to form words. Finally I say, "April 3rd is only two weeks away. Comedians take months to prepare stand-up routines."

"You've got all the material there in your vlogs. You just need to reshape it for a live audience," Hunter says. "That's all."

That's *all*? That's huge. "I can't believe you already *told* people." It's one thing to bomb in front of strangers, but to bomb in front of my friends? Are they kidding me?

"We talked to Roskinski as soon as we got the email from ITCF, and he was totally stoked," Carly says.

Roskinski is the drama teacher. Like Carly, he also thinks I need to "get out of my comfort zone."

"He booked the school bus," Carly says. "And it wasn't easy either, because there's some basketball thingy that Sunday."

A black ball of horror rises up and threatens to swamp me. "The school bus?" It holds, like, forty people.

"I know the seats have crappy springs, but we can take lots of extra coats for padding and stuff," Carly says. "It won't be so bad."

I'm not worried about the seats. I'm worried about the people sitting in the seats. All forty of them. Forty people to watch me make an ass of myself doing stand-up in front of a live audience. Forty people to come home and tell forty more, who will tell forty more, and on and on it will go. My shame will never end.

"What if I'd said no?"

"You can't afford to say no," Carly says. "And I knew you wouldn't."

She's right.

"Don't worry," Hunter adds.

"I'm not worried. I'm freaking terrified. That's three universes away from worried."

Hunter takes my hand and gives it a squeeze. "You're going to be great, Paige. You're the funniest comedian I know."

"I'm the only comedian you know."

"You're going to Portland and you'll ace the competition."

A lump the size of Mount St. Helens jams my throat.

He smiles. "And we'll be right there, watching."

I want to make a wise-ass remark, but the mountain-sized lump is cutting off my air supply. I'm going to compete in the Super Bowl of comedy. And I'm going to win.

I have no other choice.

Four

"It's a terrific opportunity for you, Paige," Dad says as we eat dinner later that night. Our kitchen smells like mashed potatoes and meatloaf. But I burned the edges of the meatloaf (as usual), and the cream I used for the potatoes was starting to go off, so there's a charred, slightly sour undertone to the air.

"Dad's right." Mom enthusiastically digs into the salad I made. She loves my salads. Everybody loves my salads. It's because they don't go near heat or dairy.

"It is. I know." Since Carly and Hunter told me the news, I've been experiencing a totally rare state called *paniness*. It's a cross between panic and happiness. Or maybe it's called *happnic*. Either way, it's so overwhelming I could puke from it.

"I told her the same thing," Grandpa says. "I am so proud of you, my little Paige note."

I push a forkful of mashed potatoes across my plate and manage a smile. Grandpa comes for dinner on Fridays when I cook and Brooke works the dinner shift at Pizza Pieman. This afternoon I showed him the email I got from the ITCF, and we spent the entire time before Mom and Dad got home talking about what a great opportunity it is. Thank God Brooke wasn't around. I don't need my sister throwing doubts at me. I'm scared enough already.

"Our Paige is going to be as famous as Kathy Griffin. Only without all the swearing and Anderson Cooper."

"Thanks, Grandpa." He has more confidence in me than I have in myself. It's touching.

"With only two weeks to prepare, you've got your work cut out for you," Mom says. "At least the pool is closed, so you don't have work on top of everything else."

One of the few physical activities I'm good at is swimming. I was hired at the community center last year to help with preschool swimming classes, but when the roof on the building started to leak in December, the whole complex was shut down for construction. I was bummed for a while—it was fun and the money was nice—but I can use the extra time now.

"You'll have to make sure your schoolwork doesn't suffer," Mom adds. "Coming up with the videos and those stand-up routines will take time."

"I do the vlogs every week, so they're no biggie." But the stand-up? Another wave of nausea grips me. Oh man. Why does that have to be part of it? "I forgot to tell you. The school drama department gets ten thousand dollars too if I win."

Dad lets out a low whistle.

"So not only is this a huge deal for me, but it's a huge deal for the school." No wonder the drama teacher was so quick to get behind it and arrange a bus. He's always complaining about being short of funds.

"Don't even think about winning," Mom says. "Just focus on doing the best job you can."

Grandpa drops his fork. It hits his plate with a loud clatter. "Oh for heaven's sake, Dina, of course she should think about winning. There's no point in entering a contest like this if you aren't in it to win."

"Yes, there is," Dad says. "In this house, we focus on enjoying the process." They are mirror images of each other: balding heads, pointy chins, bulbous brown eyes. They even frown in sync. Like they're doing right now. "It's about the experience," Dad says. "Not about the win."

"Experience, my ass," Grandpa mutters.

My parents exchange glances before Dad looks back at Grandpa. "The fact that Paige was shortlisted is an honor," he says. "She's worked hard at her comedy, and she should be proud of herself." He turns to me and smiles. "We're proud of you, kiddo. No matter what happens with the competition."

Grandpa rolls his eyes. "Of course we're proud of her. That goes without saying. But let's call a spade a spade. Paige is either in it to win or she's in it to lose. There's no point in investing all her time and energy to go down in flames."

It's a variation on Grandpa's *Life is either preparation for success or preparation for failure* line.

"I don't think—" Dad starts to say, but Grandpa is on a roll.

"Quit coddling her. If it were Brooke sitting here, you wouldn't be talking like this. You'd be telling her to go for the gold. But because it's Paige, you act like she can't walk out onstage and tell her jokes. It's as plain as the nose on your face."

Trust Grandpa to get to the point. I love that about him. I try to be like him. Only without the clichés.

"And it's just because she limps."

Mom turns the color of a radish.

Dad glares. "That's not—"

"She limps!" Grandpa repeats loudly. The words bounce off the kitchen walls. I fight an irrational urge to giggle. "Get over yourselves," he says. "And get behind your daughter!"

My parents look shocked. I almost feel sorry for them. I push back my chair. "Dessert anyone? I made a strawberry fool."

* * *

Later, when Mom and I are at the sink doing dishes, she says, "Dad and I believe in you, Paige. I hope you know that." She's up to her elbows in soap suds. I'm waiting for her to finish scrubbing the meat-loaf pan so I can dry it.

"I know. But Grandpa's right. You do coddle me." They always have. Because I was born with a clubfoot.

"We don't want you to get your hopes up and be disappointed."

"Yeah." They think I've faced so many disappointments in my life. I heard them talking about it when I was twelve. I couldn't sleep one night and I'd gotten up to get a glass of water, and they were talking about me. Feeling bad about the multiple surgeries they'd put me through when I was a toddler, the brace I'd had to wear as I grew, and the fact that the surgeries and brace hadn't worked as well as the doctors had hoped.

"No matter what happens, you'll do a wonderful job." Mom attacks a stubborn piece of burned-on meat with a scouring pad. "Dad and I can't wait to see you up on that stage."

"You can't come."

She shoots me an incredulous look. "What are you talking about? Of course we'll come."

Heat hits my cheeks. I guess I could have been more tactful about it. "This'll be the hardest thing I've ever done. It's bad enough that a pile

37

of kids from school will see me walk out on that stage. I don't want you and Dad seeing me too." Or Brooke. *Especially* Brooke.

My limp was never an issue for her when we were really little. But everything changed when we ended up in a split class together in elementary school. Instead of sticking up for me when some of the grade-five boys teased me, Brooke was embarrassed. She told me to quit walking around so much. By the end of the year she was laughing right along with them. I never knew you could love someone and hate them at the same time. But you can. I've felt that way about my sister since I was ten.

"Oh, Paige." Mom bites her lip. "I wish you didn't feel that way. I'm so sorry, honey."

There's a trace of guilt in her blue eyes. It's a look I'm familiar with. My disability isn't anything genetic. It's because Mom was low on amniotic fluid when she carried me and I hardly moved while I was in utero. Clearly my life goal to nap whenever possible was also problematic for my right foot, because I apparently squished the crap out of it for the entire nine months, and it never developed properly. Mom shouldn't feel guilty about that. I was the one sleeping on the job.

"You don't have to accept this," Mom adds. "Just because it's a terrific opportunity doesn't mean it's the right opportunity for you." She gives the pan a final rinse and hands it to me. "I'll support you whatever you decide. Whether you opt in or opt out. You know that, right?"

"I do. But I can't say no to this. I live for comedy. You know that."

I wait for her to give me the *comedy isn't a reliable way to make a living* speech, but instead she simply nods and pulls the plug from the sink.

"Winning for video comedy at the ITCF will get me agency representation," I tell her. "It'll open doors for me that I'd never be able to open myself."

"Just as long as you're sure," she says.

"I'm sure." I'm already thinking about what I'll do for my two new video bits.

She reaches for the towel. "Don't worry so much about walking out onto that stage. Concentrate on your material. Make it the best it can be. And have fun spending the money Grandpa gave you too."

"I will." He's given me three hundred dollars for clothes and to get my hair cut. "Don't worry about me, Mom. I'm going to win. And thanks to Grandpa, I'll be a winner who looks good too."

Five

'm so stoked to work on my new material that it's still dark outside when I wake up Saturday morning. I throw on a pair of sweats and go to the kitchen, where I quietly make toast and peanut butter and nuke a cup of hot chocolate. Back in my room, I lose myself for the next couple of hours working on a *First Paige Monday* vlog and then outlining a new video for the contest. By the time I'm finished, the smell of bacon is wafting underneath my bedroom door, and it's almost ten o'clock.

Ready for company and a second breakfast, I wander down the hall to the kitchen. I'm almost to the doorway when I hear my sister say, "I can't believe you'd let her do this."

I stop. Brooke knows I've been shortlisted. Of course, she's choked. She hates it when I get more attention than she does. When we were little and I had all those surgeries, she would get mad when people brought me gifts and stuff. Maybe she felt left out. I don't know.

"It's Paige's decision," Mom says. "Not ours."

"She'll totally make an ass of herself."

Really? That's what she thinks?

"I certainly hope not," Mom says.

"She'd better not say anything about me. Home stuff is off-limits."

"Paige knows that."

I do, but like Grandpa said, I'm either in it to win or I'm in it to lose. And since comedy is all about weirdness, of course I'll use my family. That's another reason I don't want Brooke or my parents there.

"Nobody thinks she's funny," Brooke says. "Some kids call her the freak."

The freak. My insides turn to mush. Brooke is the one who calls me the freak. Nobody else. I start to tremble.

"I certainly hope you stop them," Mom says sharply. "That's unacceptable."

"Of course I stop them."

Yeah right. If anybody called me a freak, my sister would probably agree. I know I should turn around and go back to my bedroom. But I don't. Instead I walk the last few steps and stop in the kitchen doorway. "Time out."

They turn to look at me. Brooke's eyes widen. Mom goes white.

I stroll to the counter, exaggerating my limp because I know it pisses my sister off. "Even freaks need their morning coffee." I pause for a heartbeat. "Hey, that could be a bumper sticker. I should get on that." And I laugh.

Because if you're laughing, you can't be sad.

*   *   *

Mom never gets involved in our fights. *You girls need to work things out yourselves,* she's always said. But this time when Brooke offers me a grudging apology, I figure Mom made her do it. I'm fine with that. I'm also fine with the fact that Brooke avoids me for most of the weekend.

That afternoon I pull out some old material that never made it to YouTube to see if anything can be rejigged for the contest, and I spend an hour commenting on a few other YouTube vlogs. It's fun to see what other people are doing, and it's a great way to boost my profile. At the mall on Sunday, I study people. It's a comedian's job to notice stuff (that's according to Chris Rock, who used a different word for *stuff*), so I spend hours observing, jotting down notes and thinking about my new routines.

I almost manage to bury Brooke's hurtful words. And so what if she doesn't think I'm funny? That's nothing new. She hasn't laughed at one of my jokes since I was ten. Anyway, Hunter believes I'm funny. I think about that when he honks his horn to pick me up for school Monday morning. Carly does too. They wouldn't have nominated me for the ITCF otherwise.

"Hey," he says when I open his car door. The smell of dark roast wraps around me like a hug.

"Hey, yourself." I slide into the passenger seat, toss my knapsack on the floor and buckle up.

He gestures to the cups in the holder between us. "I bought you an Americano when I bought mine." He shoves his rusty old Hyundai into reverse and backs out of our driveway.

"Thanks." I pop the lid on my coffee and wait for the steam to subside.

"How was your weekend?"

"Good." I look at him, and my heart does a tiny somersault. Hunter has the profile of a Roman god: perfect cheekbones, full lips, those overgrown bushy brows. Okay, so maybe the Roman gods were manscaped, but two out of three isn't bad. "How about you?"

There's a nasty grind when he puts the car into first and steps on the gas. "The same." And then he clears his throat.

Oh geez. I clutch my coffee. When he did that on Friday, he dropped a bombshell. "What?" I ask.

The light turns amber. He coasts to a stop and picks up his coffee. "You weren't at Molly's party Saturday night."

He noticed! "Nope. I was kinda busy, thanks to you and Carly." I flick a piece of lint from my jeans. "April 3rd is is only two weeks away. Do the math. That's something like 330 hours. Take away sleeping and school, and that doesn't leave much time to prep my material, figure out my clothes or work on my act." Plus, Brooke was going to that party. I didn't need that kind of hassle.

He studies me over the rim of his cup. "I figured it was because Brooke was there."

I can't lie to Hunter. He sees through me every time. "That was part of it," I admit. "But honestly, the whole idea of this competition is freaking me out. I really need to focus."

"You'll be great." The light turns green. He sticks his coffee back in the holder and steps on the gas. "I totally believe in you, Paige. I wouldn't have nominated you if I didn't."

"I'm glad." And I am. But honestly? If I had to choose between Hunter MacRae believing in me or being into me—in that *you make me want to explode* kind of way—it'd be no contest. I'd go with the explosion any day of the week.

* * *

Apparently Hunter isn't the only one who believes in me. When I get to school, I'm shocked to see a huge red-and-blue *See Paige Win* banner hanging in the foyer. And by the time I get to my locker, at least a dozen people have stopped to congratulate me.

"You're a star," Carly says when I see her on the way to math. "The whole school is behind you."

The whole school minus one. My sister.

I have drama after math, and the mood in that class is over-the-top excited.

"I can't believe you'll get a one-year contract with Endless Field," says Annalise as she sprawls on the risers, waiting for the teacher to call the class to order.

"*If* I win," I remind her.

"Of course you'll win," she says.

"And that means ten grand for the drama department too," says Liam. "Don't forget that."

"I know, right?" But as we break into small groups to refine the short pantomimed scenes we're working on, I can't miss the envy in their eyes. I get it. This is my tribe. We share the same need to step into another person's shoes, to get a reaction from an audience, to be in the spotlight. In their position, I'd be envious of my opportunity too.

"Paige," Mr. Roskinski calls when the class ends. "Can I have a word?"

"Sure."

"I don't have to tell you how thrilled I am for you," he says when he pulls up a chair beside me. With his shiny, bald head and spindly arms and legs, Mr. Roskinski has an unfortunate frog-like appearance.

"Thanks."

"But two weeks isn't much time. Especially since you need three stand-up routines."

My stomach flutters.

"And doing stand-up isn't like taping a YouTube video in your room. You can do those over and over until you're happy with them. In stand-up, you get one shot. You need to make sure you're on the mark with timing and transitions and delivery and stage presence. It's a lot to manage."

The flutter turns to a nauseous roll. Like I need the reminder? "I can do it." I *have* to do it.

"I believe you can, and I've arranged to have you excused from gym so you'll have extra time to work on your material."

"Oh wow. That's great. Thanks." Anything to miss gym. I hate that class.

"There's a lot at stake here, Paige. It's a huge opportunity for you and for the school."

Yeah, ten thousand dollars' worth of huge.

"Having a live audience is an important part of this," he adds.

Don't remind me. "I understand that. And I need to include them." I've studied enough comedians to know this. "If I exclude them, I'm dead."

He nods. "Right. But the good thing is that the audience can do half the work for you."

"What do you mean?"

"Live comedy is participatory," he says. "It relies on audience interaction. Their laughs dictate your timing. You use them to get into the flow." He lets that sink in, and then he adds, "In the meantime, I want you to use the time you'd spend in gym to develop four stand-up routines."

"I only need three."

"You need three good ones." He emphasizes the word *good.* "And because you can't always tell what will work with a given audience, you need backup material in case you need to switch gears mid-act."

That makes sense. "Okay."

"Once you get your routines down, we'll hold a trial performance here in drama. We'll do it next Monday. We'll invite some of the classes who won't be able to get to the actual competition in Portland. I'll tape you too, so you can play it back afterward, analyze your performance and see how you did."

My insides drain away. "I don't need to rehearse in drama." *In front of my friends.* "I'll be fine."

"Of course you'll rehearse." He stares at me, his buggy eyes bulging even more than usual. "Fine isn't good enough, Paige. You need to be spectacular."

Bad choice of words. I open my mouth to explain, but Mr. Roskinski isn't finished. "Think of this as an opportunity to get on top of your stage fright." He smiles. "And what better place to learn to handle it than in front of your friends."

Six

*P*aige Notes Wednesday: The problem with having a limp isn't so much that I limp; it's the fact that perfect strangers take it upon themselves to point this out to me. Like, after fifteen years I am somehow surprised by this? They also yell when they talk. Like I am deaf. HEY, YOU ARE LIMPING—DID YOU KNOW THAT? No, I didn't. And now that you've pointed it out and permanently damaged my eardrum, where's my hearing aid and crutch? Tell me that, oh wise one.

I know Mr. Roskinski is trying to help, but he's increased my stress level by about 200 percent. Doing stand-up is like auditioning in front of a bunch of strangers. But next week in drama,

I'll be doing it in front of friends. In some ways, that's worse.

Over the next couple of days, I study comedians I admire: Sarah Silverman, Amy Poehler and Margaret Cho. And in my spare time, I go to the ITCF website and check out the other nominees.

It's a big-time dumb move. I'm so shocked at how good they are, I don't have the guts to comment on a single one of their videos. So when Carly reminds me after school on Wednesday that I need something to wear onstage, I agree to go shopping with her. I'm desperate for a distraction. Anything to forget who I'm up against. But three hours of following Carly through a pile of stores is not a feel-good experience.

"Don't get discouraged," Carly says as we leave Aéropostale and walk into the mall. At least the clerk looked me in the eye when I asked for a size four in the top I liked. Half the time they treat me like I'm blind too. "We'll find you something."

Considering the fact that we've covered most of the stores at Bellevue Square Mall, I doubt it. "Maybe I'll check out the thrift store where I found those cool pants last year."

Carly wrinkles her nose. She doesn't share my taste for second-hand funk. "Not the thrift store."

"I'll buy online then." We turn the corner at Aveda. Buying online is easy, and the clerks never stare. But my order probably wouldn't arrive in time. Especially not by Monday, when I'm testing my routines in drama class. "And don't tell me you're jealous, because I know that already."

She rolls her eyes. "Rub it in, why don't you."

Carly hates that I'm a perfect size four and tall. I can't help my Swedish genes any more than she can help her pasta-loving Italian ones. Too bad Brooke inherited the Swedish hair and I got Mom's red frizz.

"Let's go in here." She stops in front of Loft.

"What? I'm a lawyer now?"

She ignores the question and heads for the elevators. "You're grumpy. You never should have gone online and looked at those other vloggers. It totally messed you up."

Technically I've been messed up since last Friday when she and Hunter dropped this bomb-shell of an opportunity on my head. Of course I'd check out the other nominees in my category.

"Athletes don't spend their time before the Super Bowl worrying about everybody else," Carly says. "They work on their own game. That's why we need to get you in game shape." She stops in front of J. Crew. "How about here? We missed it."

I shake my head. Getting me in game shape is enough to bend even my good leg out of shape. "I'm done," I say. "Let's go to Jamba Juice. I'll buy you an Orange Carrot Twist."

"I'm not thirsty. At least let's go to Sephora and deal with your hair."

We stop in front of the elevator. *Deal with your hair* is such an encouraging phrase. "Do we have to?"

She eyes the top of my head with obvious distaste. "No. Go onstage with that snarly red tumbleweed on the top of your head. I'm sure you'll get a few laughs from it."

I sigh and push the Down button.

* * *

Thursday morning, as I sit down to work in a library stall at school, I'm still traumatized by the whole Sephora experience. But considering the raw material I got, it was probably worth it.

Walking into that store was like walking into the middle of *Vogue* magazine. The women all glittered. The prices were off-the-chart stupid. And the stench of perfume made it hard to think. Or maybe it was the music affecting my brain. I couldn't hear much over it—although I definitely heard the glitter girl trying to sell me approximately $989 worth of products.

I pretty much lost all capacity to think after that.

It takes me most of the hour to jot down some notes and work it into a rough routine. I'm writing up my last few lines when a shadow looms across my cubby.

I look up. It's Ms. Vastag, wearing her infamous purple Birkenstocks and holding an armload of papers. "Why aren't you in gym class, Larsson?"

"I've been excused for a few days to practise for the competition."

Ms. Vastag's eyes narrow. "Exercise is important." She points to her ample stomach, barely covered by a tight red-and-blue-checked shirt. "Look what happens when you don't get it."

"I know, and I feel terrible about missing the class, but I need the time."

Ms. Vastag glances around and then leans close. "You don't fool me for a minute. You hate gym." She glances at my leg. "You're always looking for an excuse to sit it out because of your disability."

Ms. Vastag doesn't dance around my limp like so many people do. And she doesn't make allowances for it either. She treats me with the same offhand annoyance she treats everybody else with. I like that about her.

She's not finished. "You can't run from reality."

"I can't run, period."

The ghost of a smile flashes at the corners of her mouth. "Maybe not a marathon, but you can manage. And here's the thing. Everybody has something. A deformed foot, a brother in jail, bad gas. Whatever. Life's a poker hand. We all have to deal. But the bigger person learns not to be defined by the hand they hold. Speaking of holding..." She thrusts a piece of paper at me. "The *Seattle Times* wants you to call."

My heart skips a beat as I look down at the small slip of paper. *Dylan Shaw, Seattle Times*

Entertainment is written in thick black ink. The name is followed by a phone number. "Me?"

That hint of a smile is back. "I assume so. Unless there's another Paige Larsson around here." She turns to go. "You can call him after school. You've got work to do. And that's no laughing matter."

* * *

When God handed out patience, I was clearly napping, because I have none.

A reporter from the *Seattle Times* wants to talk to *me*. I can't wait until after school. But I can't skip math either, so I wait until class is over, and when the bell rings I hurry down the hall to the band wing. After a couple of jocks finish at their lockers, I punch out the number Ms. Vastag gave me.

"Dylan Shaw."

His voice is brisk. I hear someone talking behind him. Maybe he's busy. Maybe I should I have waited until after school?

"Hi. This is Paige Larsson." I sound like a mouse running laps. I take a deep breath. "I'm returning your call." Oh God, now I sound like an uptight secretary.

"Right. Hi. Thanks for calling. And congratulations on being shortlisted for the International Teens in Comedy Festival."

"Thanks." I figured on some publicity, but I didn't figure on it before the event.

"My boss wants me to do a feature on it for the weekend paper."

My breath stalls. A feature! In the weekend paper! Brooke loves the fashion and entertainment section. She loves, loves, loves it. And this week I'll be in it. Maybe now she'll take my comedy seriously. My knees start to tremble. I lean against a locker for support. The gray steel is cold through my thin T-shirt.

"Since you and another teen from Washington State are going to the competition, I thought I'd get quotes from each of you."

"Sure." It's like I'm channelling Carly, or maybe I'm just remembering what she said to me last Friday, but I manage to answer all his questions without sounding like a mouse or a secretary or anything else embarrassing. It helps that Dylan is easy to talk to and that he quotes the guy from Spokane who made the shortlist in the straight stand-up category.

"Your YouTube vlogs are great, by the way."

"Thanks." I wonder if he really checked them out or if he's just saying that.

"I'd like to pull a visual from the one you did on dating a toaster to run with the article. Would you be okay with that?"

He *has* watched them. I had Carly film me while I took my toaster out for pizza and to the movies. Me and toaster boy even went for a romantic walk in the park at the end of the night. And before I started editing, I searched through my royalty-free music file for something really romantic to mix in. It was so good that even I laughed when I played it back. "Sure."

"Judging by how funny they are," he adds, "I'd say you have a great chance of winning."

Seven

Saturday morning, I wake up to the sound of a crow being slaughtered.

Heart pounding, I bolt out from under my covers and stare around my room. Was I was dreaming? Then I hear it again—the silly Ricky Gervais bird ringtone I downloaded last month.

It's my phone. I forgot to set it to *Silent* when I went to bed last night. Grabbing it from the nightstand, I slide back under the covers and peer through sleep-crusted eyes at the screen.

Three text messages and one missed call. All from Hunter.

For him, I'll wake up to the sound of slaughtered crows any day of the week. I bunch my pillow up under my head and hit *Redial*.

"What is wrong with you?" I ask when he answers. "It's not even seven thirty yet." So what if I'm happy to hear from him? I can't let him know that.

"I take it you're still in bed?"

I flush. There's something incredibly intimate about his voice whispering in my ear while I'm lying half naked under the covers. Even if I am wearing a ripped *Friends* T-shirt that has a big ketchup stain across Jennifer Aniston's face. "Of course I'm still in bed."

"So you haven't seen the *Seattle Times*?"

"Since I haven't quite mastered the whole reading-in-my-sleep thing yet, that would be a no."

"There's a huge picture of you on the front of today's entertainment section," he says. "Come downstairs and answer your front door. I bought three extra copies."

And the doorbell rings.

* * *

Okay, so my picture isn't *that* huge. And I'm not the only one on the front of the entertainment section either. The guy from Spokane, Jacob Muller, is beside me. But Dylan Shaw has repeated his pronouncement that he expects me to win. He has compared me to Amy Poehler. *In his first paragraph.* Hunter thinks I should be ecstatic. Instead I'm numb. I'm nowhere close to Poehler. She's, like, up in the stratosphere. I'm somewhere down in middle earth, trying to crawl my way out.

Hunter looks up from his phone. "The number of your subscribers just went up again." He's sprawled on the couch in the TV room, and I'm in Dad's ratty old easy chair across from him, a copy of the paper spread out at my feet. On the coffee table between us are the two Americanos Hunter brought over, along with an almost empty bag of All Dressed potato chips and a couple of raspberry muffins. "You've got over seventy-five hundred."

Whoa! That's two thousand more than I had last night when I went to bed. All because of an article in the *Seattle Times.* My phone buzzes. **Your subscribers are going up BY THE MINUTE**, Carly texts. **You are already famous**.

What I am is shocked. This whole morning feels unreal. "I can't believe this."

Hunter digs out the last few chips. "Believe it." His dark hair is sticking up on one side of his head, like he hasn't combed it properly or hasn't showered yet this morning. Or like he was in a hurry to drive over and see me. My tummy does a tiny flip-flop.

Don't be stupid. As I fold the newspaper sections into one neat pile, I hear voices coming from the kitchen. Mom and Dad? Mom and Brooke? I can't tell. At least Mom was up when Hunter rang the bell, which gave me a few minutes to throw myself together. *Throw* being the operative word. When I came downstairs in my jeans and sweater, Hunter calmly pointed out that I had a bright-red streak of something on my chin. It was blush. That's what I get for trying to multitask before breakfast.

C U tomorrow, Carly adds. **11:30. DON'T forget**.

How could I? The salon—Fringe Benefits— has called *and* emailed to remind me of my hair appointment.

Hunter tosses his phone aside, grabs the empty potato-chip bag and crumples it up. "Why don't we go out?" he suggests. "Grab something to eat? My treat."

Hunter is always asking me to go places. I never used to mind. But last year, when my feelings went through that change, it started to feel awkward. I want to go *out* out with him, not just hang out.

"If you're hungry, have one of the muffins."

"I'd rather drive over to Big June's for her stuffed French toast. Come with me. You love her cinnamon buns."

Of course I do. What's not to love? They're the size of a dinner plate and loaded with enough sugar to send you into a diabetic coma. That's the other problem. Not diabetic comas (I always order a side of scrambled eggs, and I'm pretty sure the protein cancels out the sugar), but the fact that everybody loves them. Big June's is a popular place. I don't want to walk in there with Hunter and see someone from school. "I can't. I have a ton to do before Monday." I rattle off my list: haircut, clothes, the second video I need for the contest. "Plus, I have to get my routine ready for the practice run in drama."

He stands up, slides his phone away and shoves his feet into his runners. "Yeah, I heard about that." Instead of heading for the front door, he turns toward the kitchen. I'm confused until I spot the empty chip bag in his hand. He's going to throw it away before he leaves. Hunter hates litter as much as I hate germs. What a team we'd make. For sure we'd live in a clutter-free, sterile environment. How romantic is that?

"Roskinski's telling everybody," he adds.

I roll my eyes as we walk down the hall. "Great."

His chuckle is low and soft. So sexy. My heart races a little. "I figured you'd be impressed," he says.

The voices in the kitchen grow louder as we get closer. My shoulder blades tighten. It's not Mom talking. It's Brooke and Twin One. Or maybe Twin Two. Whatever. The twin part doesn't matter. The Brooke part does. To give her fair warning that we're coming, I clear my throat and say in a too-loud voice, "The garbage is in here."

Hunter looks at me as if I've suddenly turned into an owl. "I know where your garbage is."

The voices stop when we reach the doorway. Brooke and Twin One are sitting at the kitchen table, drinking coffee. They look over and smile. The paper is open between them. I see a large coffee stain on the picture of my face. Coincidence? I don't think so.

"Hey, Brooke," Hunter says as he heads for the trash can.

"Hey, yourself," Brooke drawls. There's enough syrup in her voice to send anybody into a diabetic coma. "You're looking hot."

Hunter always looks hot. And whenever Brooke sees him, she points it out. If I didn't know better, I'd say my sister has a thing for him. Except she likes college guys with tricked-out cars. Her current target drives a silver Audi.

"Thanks." His shoulders flex as he pitches his empty bag into the garbage. He really is rocking that tight black T-shirt.

"Pour yourself some java and grab a chair," Brooke says. She doesn't even look at me. No surprise.

"Thanks, but I'm heading out." He gestures to the paper. "Great article, right?"

"Yeah." Brooke smirks. She looks at Twin One. "We were just discussing that and the whole contest thing."

Twin One grows very still. Her face fills with color. I'm suddenly on alert, waiting for the bomb to drop. Hunter, oblivious to the undercurrents, walks back toward me.

"It's good that the ITCF is making space for people with disabilities this year," Brooke says.

I turn cold. At least she's being politically correct. She hasn't called me a freak once yet this morning. Twin One inspects her nails and won't meet my gaze.

Brooke slides a quick sideways glance at me before giving Hunter a brilliant smile. "It's great for their image. It's probably part of their mandate that they have to include them or something."

Them. Nice one, Brooke.

"You know. Make a few spaces for the 'disabled.'" She puts air quotes around the word *disabled.*

Hunter clears his throat. His eyes harden. "That's not very—"

"Smart," I interrupt. I am furious. Embarrassing me in front of Hunter is a new low. "You'd think they'd have special categories for people like me. Para-comedy or something."

Twin One snickers. When Brooke shoots her a warning look, she picks up her coffee and hides behind her cup.

"You should get on that, Brookie." Brooke hates it when I call her that. I take Hunter's arm and tug him out of the kitchen. "Write them a letter. Include your title too. MRO of Larsson Enterprises."

Hunter bursts out laughing. Twin One snorts coffee out of her nose. My sister looks confused. She obviously missed the *Paige Notes* vlog I did two Wednesdays ago, where I ranted about telemarketers and called them MROs, which is short for major rectal opening. Too bad for her.

"Did you just call your sister an asshole?" Hunter asks as we head down the hall.

"No way. I wouldn't stoop so low." I dredge up a wide smile, even though inside I am dying. That black pit of self-hate is back, and it takes everything I have not to get sucked in. "Major rectal opening is the official, scientific term." I open the door with an exaggerated flourish. "And I'm all about being scientific."

I watch him walk down the steps. He's still laughing when he gets to his car.

It's a small victory. But a good one.

Eight

First Paige Monday: The word for the week is porcelain. *Porcelain is big in my house. My mom's a dentist, and my dad's a plumber. They're all about the teeth and the toilets. If my sister and I brush and flush, they're happy. Conversation at dinner is a little problematic though. I can never figure out what opening they're talking about. The mouth or the toilet. Talk about potty mouth.*

Dad's van hits a pothole when he slows for the school zone. On the sidewalk, students in groups of twos and threes straggle down the block to school. Since Hunter has a doctor's appointment, Dad's driving me this morning.

"Good luck with your dry run in drama today." Dad leans over and pats my knee.

I lick my suddenly dry lips. A knee tap is big-time encouragement coming from Dad. "Thanks."

He turns into the drop-off zone. I see a couple of Brooke's friends up ahead, including Twin Two. Oh crap. At least Brooke isn't there. She's pretty much avoided me since Saturday morning. Maybe I should call her a major rectal opening more often.

I fling open the passenger door. "This is good."

"Whoa. Hold up." He slams on the brakes. "You'll hurt yourself."

"Yeah. If I wrecked my good foot that would be disastrous." Almost as bad as being driven to school by a parent. "Thanks, Dad." I grab my bag and jump out before any of Brooke's friends see me.

I'm halfway to my locker when Carly calls out, "Paige, wait!"

I stop in front of the basketball team's trophy cabinet and watch her hurry down the hall, her dark hair streaming out behind her and a wide smile on her face.

Her smile fades when she stops in front of me. "What are you wearing?" She stares at the flowing peach top I picked up at the thrift store yesterday after I got my hair cut. I also found a cool vest and scored a pair of nearly new 7 For All Mankind black jeans. "I thought you were wearing something red for this afternoon's performance."

Carly believes in color therapy. She thinks red will energize me and draw positive attention. To get her own positive attention, she relies on tight, low-cut sweaters in every color going. Today's is royal blue. "I changed my mind."

She frowns. "Not smart. Peach stimulates the appetite."

"That's good." We start to walk. "I'll leave them hungry for more."

Nothing can spoil my mood. Yesterday's haircut turned out okay (my hair looks almost normal for the first time in, like, forever). My routines are feeling solid, and the subscription numbers on my YouTube channel are up. Way up.

"I almost reached nine thousand subscribers this morning," I tell Carly. It's low by Jenna Marbles standards, but great considering I've only been doing this for nine months.

She grins. "I saw. I'll bet you'll hit that magic ten thousand before we leave for Portland at the end of the week. Maybe then you'll start making some money."

I stop in front of my locker. My hands are clammy. It takes me a couple of tries to spin my combination. "Maybe." I don't know why I'm resisting turning this into a business. Maybe because until now, vlogging has been fun. And chasing money makes it more serious somehow.

She turns to go. "See you at lunch."

"Don't count on it. Roskinski wants to see me in the drama room."

"I'll be in the caf. Come find me when you're done."

But I don't. By the time Mr. Roskinski finishes explaining how the afternoon will work, there's only twenty minutes left until the first bell. He disappears to the staff room, and I eat my cheese sandwich sitting on the risers, staring at the stage. I'll be performing twice in last block to four different classes. Thank goodness Brooke's class isn't one of them.

The stage curtains are half open. Mr. Roskinski has turned on a single spotlight. Most of the other lights in the room are off, throwing the stage into sharp relief. I don't let myself think about Portland, the ITCF or what's at stake with the contest. Instead, I visualize myself walking out from behind that shabby gold curtain, delivering my lines and hearing the laughter.

That's all I focus on: the laughter.

When the bell goes, I spend first block in the library, reviewing my notes. I've memorized both routines, but in light of what Mr. Roskinski said about having backup material, I've also got a few bits I can pull out in case I need them. By the time last block rolls around and I head back to the classroom, I'm stoked. I'm ready.

Or I think I am. But as I stand backstage listening to seventy students coming into the room, I realize I should have brought my antiperspirant to school. I look like I have two peaches blooming under my armpits.

When Mr. Roskinski calls my name, my heart skips a beat. I clutch the wireless mic in my slippery palms and leave the wings. I don't look at him, though I know he's standing off to the side, recording every second of my performance.

"Walk much?" I ask as I limp to the front of the stage. I hear a few nervous giggles. But when I add, "Not really," the laughing starts.

That gives me the confidence I need to start on my bit about my trip to Sephora, which doesn't get the number of laughs I expect. Different jokes work with different groups—comedy rule number two. And there are way more guys than girls in this group. My panic starts to rise. I glance at Mr. Roskinski, who gestures to his pocket. Our signal for *pull out something else.*

"I am so over body odor," I say, segueing into a piece I wrote on a whim last night. "I mean, what was God thinking? Why couldn't she have designed our sweat to smell like bacon? Or banana cupcakes?" The laughs start again, and though my pacing isn't great, the laughs keep coming for the rest of the routine. Afterward, as those two classes leave and the next two classes file in, Mr. Roskinski talks to me backstage.

"Don't be afraid to slow down a little and leave time for the audience to laugh," he says. "And glance around the group more too."

That'll be tough. I've been focusing on one or two friendly faces. Since Hunter and Carly and a few of my other friends are in this next group, I figured I'd focus on them.

I also figured I'd be less nervous this time too. Wrong. I'm practically hyperventilating as I wait for Mr. Roskinski to introduce me. Maybe because Hunter and Carly and some of my friends *are* in this group. When he calls my name, I momentarily blank out. But when he gestures with his hand, I snap back and start to move.

"Walking is great exercise," I say when I reach the middle of the stage. "Unless you're me." A couple of nervous titters. "Maybe that's why my parents named me Paige and named my sister Brooke." The laughter starts to build. It's an easy shot because people in this group know Brooke. They can relate. "I mean, how fast can a page move, you know what I'm saying?" More laughter. "Brooks are like small rivers, so they don't have that problem. They're always on the move. Even if they are a little shallow."

Everybody laughs.

Okay, maybe it's a low blow, but it's the only joke I'll make today about Brooke, and it gives me the confidence I need. Forcing myself to gaze at the entire group, I slow down and let the laughter dictate when to deliver the next line. My Sephora material goes over way better with this crowd, and my rant about self-checkout counters at the supermarket makes them laugh too. I end with my funny bit about sleeping on the job while I was in utero and "being born wrong." Before I know it, I have four peaches blooming under my armpits, and my second practice run is over.

"That was great!" Carly says when she and Hunter come up to me afterward. A few students are hanging out talking, but the rest have left. Mr. Roskinski is sitting at his desk, writing something. Carly nudges Hunter. "Right?"

"Yeah. You did great." But his voice is flat, his face weirdly blank. And he just cleared his throat.

I stare at him. "What's wrong? And don't tell me nothing, because that would be a lie."

A hit of color blooms high on his cheeks. "It was a cheap shot, that's all."

Irritation prickles the back of my neck. "Oh come on! You know what Brooke's been saying about me. You heard her on Saturday. What I said about her today was nothing." Especially compared to what I plan to say about her at the competition.

"I'm not talking about Brooke," Hunter says. "She's just being a jealous bag."

A bag, yes. Jealous? I don't think so.

"I'm talking about you," he adds. "The way you made fun of yourself. It was stupid."

My breath catches. "It wasn't stupid. The audience laughed. That means it worked."

"Whatever." But he won't meet my gaze. "I thought it was dumb."

There's a funny pressure behind my eyes. Dumb? Really? Before I can answer, he turns away. I spot Mr. Roskinski walking toward me.

"You did great," Carly mouths. She gestures to Hunter's back. "He's wrong."

Carly's right. It wasn't dumb. I'm onstage to get laughs. No matter what it takes.

Nine

C omedy isn't just telling a joke. It's timing, it's setup, it's facial expressions, it's choosing the right topic. Over the next few days I eat, sleep and breathe my routines. I watch the sessions Mr. Roskinski taped so many times I can practically recite them in my sleep. I analyze every word I speak, every pause I make, every beat of laughter I get back. I try out new lines and tweak the existing ones. I visualize a perfect delivery. I try on my stage clothes, pack and repack my suitcase. Wednesday, I email my two video submissions to the contest organizers. Thursday, I do another dry run in drama, only this time I do it after school and Mr. Roskinski is the only one watching, which is weird because he doesn't laugh once, but I have to pause anyway, as if he is.

"Remember to breathe, to take your time and to let the energy build as you get into your set," Mr. Roskinski says after I finish. "Now go home and get a good night's sleep so you're well rested for tomorrow's drive to Portland."

Since I was pretty much born to sleep, I don't expect to have trouble sleeping Thursday night. And I don't. I fall asleep soon after I go to bed, and it's all good until my eyes fly open and I wake up in a cold sweat at 3:37 AM.

I'm competing in the ITCF. *And I cannot fail.*

It takes me hours to doze back off. And then I sleep through my alarm, which means I'm still in bed when Hunter comes to the door to pick me up. Hunter can't stick around, but luckily Mom has the day off so she gets my breakfast, helps me pack my toiletries and drives me to school. I spend block one in math pretending I'm concentrating, and block two in the library pretending I'm reviewing my material. In reality, I'm obsessing. All I can think of is how big a deal this is and how scared I am. Finally, at ten to eleven, I put my material away and head for my locker.

Where R U? Carly texts as I check and recheck the bag I checked and rechecked last night and again this morning. I'm terrified I've forgotten my antiperspirant. No way do I want to sweat peaches on stage again. **Hurry up**, she adds.

I glance at my watch. We're leaving at eleven. I still have five minutes. **Relax**, I text back. **Roskinski's not on board yet anyway**. I see him down the hall, standing outside the office talking to Ms. Vastag.

Hunter saved you a seat. :)

In that case...I zip up my bag, slam my locker shut and head down the hall. As I pass the office, Ms. Vastag looks over and smiles. Whoa. I almost stumble. Last time she smiled, I was in grade eight. "Good luck, Paige."

Paige? Now she's calling me *Paige*?

"We're all rooting for you."

It's the nicest thing Vastag has ever said to me. It's also the scariest. Because it tells me how much is riding on my win.

Outside, a light drizzle is falling—the misty, barely there kind that does a real number on my hair. I tuck as much of it as I can under my raincoat and hurry down the sidewalk to the yellow bus waiting at the end of the drop-off zone.

I'm not even to the back of the bus when the cheering starts. "Larsson, Larsson..."

My face flames. *Oh God, kill me now.*

When I reach the side of the bus, I see it: a six-foot-long paper banner taped to the side windows. Huge red letters say *Comedy star Paige Larsson goes for the win.* And ITCF *rules!*

Comedy star? Seriously? It's not enough that I'm about to potentially humiliate myself onstage in front of hundreds of strangers, but I have to humiliate myself for three hours on I-5 getting there?

Smiling, the driver takes my bag and stows it with the other luggage. I take a deep breath and step onto the bus. The claps and whistles start. I spot Annalise and Liam. More buddies from drama. Hunter and Carly. Everybody's smiling. My throat tightens. These guys are my friends. And they're totally, 100 percent behind me. I'm lucky. I grin. "Gimp coming through."

"Larsson, Larsson!" The cheers keep coming.

How embarrassing. "Shut up, guys, you're violating the noise bylaws." I make my way down the aisle. "They're already getting calls in the office." Clearly nobody believes me, because the cheers keep coming. I slide into the empty seat beside Hunter. An open bag of potato chips sits on his knees.

Across the aisle, Carly is grinning like a crazy fool. "Oh my god, Paige, I can't believe this day has finally come!" She fist-pumps the air.

"Yeah. It's amazing how Friday comes after Thursday." I start to pull my jacket off. "I can hardly believe it myself."

Carly rolls her eyes. Hunter sets aside his chips to help me with my sleeve. There's a chip crumb on his lower lip. I wonder what it would be like to kiss it away. Or have the guts to tell him how I feel. The thought makes me hot.

"Sleep much?" he teases.

"As much as possible."

He laughs. "At least you're relaxed about everything."

"I'm so relaxed, I can barely keep my eyes open." I open my mouth to fake a yawn, and a real yawn takes over.

Carly leans over and sticks her phone under my nose. "I told you you'd hit that ten-thousand mark."

I stare down at the screen. It takes me a second to make sense of what I'm seeing. My YouTube channel has ten thousand subscribers. Before I was shortlisted for the ITCF, I had five thousand. "Wow." My mouth is suddenly dry. "This whole thing has been totally worth it." All the practicing, all the stressing.

"Of course it's been worth it," Hunter says.

"And it's only the beginning," Carly says. "Because you're going to win, and you'll go to New York, and you'll be a star."

Annalise leans over from the seat ahead of us. "And the drama department will get ten grand out of the deal too!" she says.

My heart lurches. "I know. It's gonna be great!" As long as I win. If I lose, I let everybody down.

A few minutes later, Mr. Roskinski boards the bus and the driver slides into his seat. After a reminder about proper bus etiquette (no cheering, no standing, no walking around) and an announcement that we're stopping for lunch in Centralia, which is midway between Seattle and Portland, we head off.

But by the time the bus hits I-5 south, I almost forget about the ITCF. Partly because the stupid springs on the bus seats make thinking impossible and partly because I'm sitting beside Hunter and the lack of springs means we're constantly bumping shoulders.

And shoulder bumping Hunter as we drive down I-5 is enough to make any girl forget her worries.

Everything's good until we reach Portland.

"In another minute or so, we'll be driving by the Arlene Schnitzer Concert Hall," Mr. Roskinski says. "It'll be on the right-hand side of the street."

I stare out the window. The traffic on Southwest Broadway is heavy. We're barely creeping along.

"There it is," someone shouts.

I spot the long green *Portland* sign attached to the side of the building. It looks like a giant pen. As the bus inches forward, the marquee comes into view: *The International Teens in Comedy Festival. Welcome to America's Newest & Funniest. Sponsored by Acacia Communications.*

My stomach erupts. Not into dainty butterflies but into a mess of rabid bats. This is really happening.

"You guys are headliners," Carly says. "That's so cool."

"Hey." Hunter nudges me. "Isn't that your dad by the entrance?"

"No way." I lean forward so I can see around Carly's shoulder. "It can't be."

I blink once, twice, three times. It's Dad, all right. He's standing in front of the marquee, one arm around Mom and the other around Grandpa, a big smile on his face.

Oh no. No, no, no. This can't be happening.

And then I spot the person taking the picture, and all hell breaks loose in the bat kingdom of my stomach. It's Brooke. She's standing between Twin One and Twin Two.

Ten

"**G**randpa insisted on it," Mom says about thirty minutes later when we're sitting on butter-yellow leather chairs in the hotel lobby. Across from me, Grandpa beams with pride. "He made all the arrangements," Mom adds. "He booked our rooms at the hotel. He contacted the festival office to make sure we'd have tickets waiting at the box office. He even arranged to borrow Jerry's nine-seater van so we could all drive down together."

Grandpa is a make-it-happen kind of guy. Normally I love it. Today, not so much.

The lobby is crowded. People are clustered by the tour desk, the entrance to the bar, the gift shop. There's a steady stream of bodies coming through the circular front doors and heading for the check-in desk too. Most of them are around my age. Most of them are trailing suitcases. And most of them have that same *is this for real?* look of panic in their eyes.

My competition.

"We wanted to show up and surprise you!" Grandpa says.

Surprises like this I don't need. I'd literally just finished checking in—I hadn't even been to my room yet—and when I turned around from reception, there they were. At least, Mom, Dad, and Grandpa were there. Brooke and the twins were in the gift shop.

"We haven't been taking your comedy aspirations seriously enough." Dad rubs his eyes. I can tell the drive from Seattle has exhausted him. Grandpa's a terrible backseat driver. "We wanted to be here to support you."

"And I know you're nervous and you'd rather we didn't watch, but just don't think about us being in the audience." Mom picks up my hand and gives it a squeeze. "Okay?" When I don't answer, she squeezes my hand a second time and says, "You'll do great, Paige."

"Yeah, great." I drag the word out—*griiiiiiiiit.* Maybe they'll think I'm pretending to be southern and not realize I'm having trouble talking between gritted teeth. I clutch my welcome package and force myself to look happy. They mean well. They do.

I just wish they could mean well from home.

"You're staying on the concierge floor." Mom smiles. "We tried to get on your floor, but they wouldn't let us."

Thank God for small mercies. "The tenth floor has been reserved for contestants." Having my own room is a perk and probably a blessing too, although it would have been fun to room with Carly. But she and Hunter and the other kids are two floors down.

"And the hotel has a shuttle," Dad adds. "So you won't have to walk to and from the concert hall. Your mother checked."

"I know. They told me."

"But we can't let you take the shuttle tomorrow morning," Grandpa says. "We'll drive you ourselves."

"You don't need to do that."

"Of course we don't, but we will."

I'm actually relieved. Going into the theater tomorrow morning will be scary, and it'll be nice

to have my family beside me. My mind flashes on Brooke. Okay, *some* of my family beside me.

"We want to be there every step of the way," Grandpa adds.

Nodding, I glance around the lobby. A slim woman wearing leather pants and a royal-purple cape jacket is coming through the circular doors. Something about her looks familiar. She turns to the man beside her and laughs. My heart skips a beat.

Holy crap, it's Raven Prest!

She saunters toward the reception desk, a soft-sided leather bag slung over one shoulder, chatting casually to her companion. She's taller than I expected and totally glammed out with poppy-red lipstick and sleek, short black hair.

"...join us for dinner tonight," Grandpa is saying. The elevator in my stomach bottoms out. Oh no. I look back at him. "Your mom and dad. Brooke and the twins. I've made a reservation at a local steak house. My treat, of course."

"I have the reception at the concert hall. They're sending shuttles to pick us up at five thirty." We're expected to tour backstage so we'll know what to expect tomorrow, and the sponsors and judges are being introduced afterward.

"It ends at seven," Grandpa says. "I asked. So I made the reservation for eight."

I don't want to see my family afterward. Being around them—around Brooke—will totally throw me off. "I'm seeing Hunter and Carly after," I tell him. "But thanks."

"They can come too," Grandpa says. "I'm sure the restaurant can accommodate a few extra people."

Oh man. A mixture of love and exasperation rolls through me. "Thanks, Grandpa, but Carly's picked out a place she wants to try." I'm desperate enough to lie.

Grandpa throws up his hands. "Well then, I'll cancel the steak house and we can go where Carly wants."

Why does he have to be so easygoing? "It's a sushi place," I blurt out. Grandpa and Dad hate sushi. "That's all they have—a *ton* of sushi." I need to text Carly and bring her up to speed before she runs into Grandpa in the hall and blows my lie out of the water.

Grandpa frowns. "They can't just have fish. Too many people have allergies."

"They do. It's a Japanese place." Panic sends my voice into squeaky-mouse territory. "Raw fish all the way."

"Surely they'll have rice. The Japanese eat lots of rice. And all those delicious deep-fried things with that sweet dipping sauce. I can't remember the name."

"Tempura," Dad offers helpfully.

I glare at him, but he's looking at Grandpa.

"That's it! Tempura. And we can get one of those private rooms!" Grandpa's cheeks are flushed with enthusiasm. "I love those little rooms. Even if they do make you take your shoes off before you get in."

The air disappears from my lungs. This can't be happening. I know I should be grateful, but I don't want them here. For sure I don't want to see them tonight. As I'm scrambling for another excuse, Mom says, "You know, Dad, Paige shouldn't have to change her plans for us. Especially the night before the big event. Why don't we let her see her friends tonight and we can go out tomorrow night?"

I shoot Mom a grateful look.

"What, we're not going for dinner tonight?" says a familiar voice from behind me.

It's Brooke. I swivel around. She's carrying a small gold bag from the gift shop and standing between Twin One and Twin Two. I stare at their feet. Who wears stilettos? With *jeans*? Especially when it's raining? The three of them do, obviously. My jaw tightens. I'd give my right foot to be able to wear stilettos. Seriously. I'd be thrilled to get rid of the thing.

"Paige can't make it," Mom says.

Brooke pouts. "Oh, that's too bad." It's a real pout. A *genuine* one. The ice around my heart starts to thaw. My sister actually wants me there for dinner.

"We were looking forward to the steak house." She looks at the twins. "Right, girls?"

"Right." Said in unison. With synchronized nods. Like little soldiers answering to their general.

"Well then," Dad says. "We'll go to the steak house tonight, and we'll find someplace else for tomorrow night. Because tomorrow night we'll be celebrating the fact that Paige made the finals." His voice is laced with pride. "And that deserves a special dinner too."

Like, no pressure. As I try to figure out what to say to that, Brooke adds, "Oh good. I wouldn't want to miss celebrating Paige's crack at the big time." But her smile is brittle, and there's a vaguely sarcastic inflection to her words. "I'm so glad I'm here to see it."

Sure she is. The ice around my heart hardens again. I know the truth. Brooke has come to Portland to watch me fail.

Eleven

The shuttle drops me outside the Arlene Schnitzer Concert Hall at quarter to six. My heart does a jumping-jack routine when I see the crowds on the sidewalk and the marquee blazing with lights. It reminds me of Broadway. Plastering a smile on my face, I join the people lining up to get in. At least tonight all I have to do is listen and blend with the crowd. But tomorrow...

Don't go there.

Forcing myself to stay in the moment, I study the people around me. Most of them are gazing awkwardly into space, trying to avoid eye contact. I check out their clothes. At least I've hit the right note of casual chic in my dressy black pants, midnight-blue chiffon top and jeweled flats.

"Excuse me." A plump guy with hair the color of maple syrup materializes at my side. He's wearing wire-rimmed glasses and a slouchy tweed jacket. A bright-orange name tag hangs from his neck. The same kind I'm wearing. A contestant's name tag. "Aren't you Paige Larsson?"

It takes me a second to place him. He's the teen comic from Spokane who was featured in the newspaper article with me. "You're Jacob Muller." The muscles in my shoulders loosen a little. It's great to see a familiar face. Even if it's a face I've never actually met. "Talk about good timing."

"I'm all about the timing," he says solemnly. And we both crack up.

As we make our way to the front door, we compare notes on who we came with (he drove with his parents), where we're staying (he has an uncle in town) and our worries about tomorrow.

"My straight stand-up category starts at eight thirty," he says. "You video guys aren't on until eleven. At least you can sleep in."

"I doubt I'll be doing much of that."

After a woman checks our names off a list, we're ushered past a white-and-gold *Welcome to* the 15ᵗʰ *Annual Teens in Comedy Festival* sign and into the lobby. Crystal chandeliers hang over a shiny checkerboard floor. An elegant staircase sweeps up to a mezzanine crowded with people. My mouth turns dry. That's a long walk. And I've never been great on stairs.

A guy about our age steps forward. He's wearing thick black glasses and a burgundy blazer with a small silver usher pin on his lapel. "I'm Drew," he says. "If you'll follow me, I'll show you the theater before taking you backstage."

The theater is as beautiful as the lobby, with its grand balcony and incredible vintage detail. I spot other ushers showing contestants around, but I can't tell if they're in my category. They're too far ahead and the lighting is too muted to make out facial features.

Drew leads us past plush bluish-purple seats, filling us in on the building's historic past before going into the specifics of where everyone will sit this weekend. "Judges, officials and the media will sit in the front rows." He stops about twenty rows from the stage beside section A. "You and your friends and family will sit here. You'll get your seat numbers in a few minutes."

"My category doesn't start until eleven, and my welcome package said I don't need to arrive until ten o'clock," I tell him. "Do I come into the theater?"

"Nice way to be supportive," Jacob mutters. But he's smiling.

"There'll be ushers at the main entrance when you arrive." Drew leads us down another aisle to a side door. "Identify yourself to one of them, and they'll take you backstage."

We follow him down a hall and past a series of closed doors to an open doorway. "This is the main dressing room," he says. "Tomorrow you'll wait here for your name to be called." Tonight it's a blur of people, wardrobe racks, makeup stations and random chairs.

An older woman with brilliant red hair asks us for our names. Seconds later she hands us each an envelope. "You'll find your seat number in there," Drew says as he steers us out the door and back down the hall. "It's good for both days— plus there are drink tickets for the mezzanine upstairs. You can head up to the reception after I'm done showing you around." He grins. "Don't even bother asking the bartender for booze. You won't get it. But they have lots of soda."

When he stops beside a door marked *Stage*, my heart skips a beat. This is where it'll all happen. "You'll always have an escort, so don't worry about finding your way around. An usher will bring you down here five minutes before you're due to go on." He opens the door. Nerves thrumming, I follow him and Jacob into the wings.

The lighting backstage is dim. Cables snake across the floor. Fist-sized clumps of wires curl up the walls. Tracks of lights and booms hang from scaffolding overhead. A few guys wearing crew T-shirts are huddling by a computer station. Drew leads us over to a couple of other ushers standing beside a red velvet curtain. "You'll wait here until you're introduced. And I know we're talking tonight, but obviously tomorrow you're expected to be quiet."

I peer over his shoulder. The spotlight is on center stage. Two teens—a guy and a girl—are standing in front of a microphone, looking straight ahead. Oh crap. He doesn't expect us to walk out there *now*, does he?

The teens walk back to the wings. I stare at them as they go past. I don't recognize the girl, but I'm pretty sure the guy is in my category.

"Your turn," Drew says. "Walk out and get a feel for it."

It's my worst nightmare come to life. "I'm good," I say. "Really. I'll wait until tomorrow." I know I'm being stupid. If I can't walk onstage tonight, when no one is watching, how will I walk out tomorrow, when everyone is? But I'm suddenly überself-conscious of my limp, of how I must look.

"Come on," Jacob says. His face is the color of milk, and perspiration shines above his top lip. "Don't make me go out there alone."

Heat creeps up my neck. I need to get over myself. Jacob is too busy being nervous to care how I look when I walk. "Okay."

Jacob matches his pace to mine as we walk to center stage. A bead of sweat trickles down my back as I stare into the empty theater. The spotlight is hotter than I expected. The theater lights are on, and even with the spotlight shining into my eyes, I can see every single empty seat.

Tomorrow they'll be full.

"You good?" Jacob asks.

There are nineteen others in my category. In terms of skill, I figure I'm about midrange. "Not as good as some, but better than others."

He snickers. "I meant, are you good to go?"

The heat races from my neck into my cheeks. "Yeah, I'm good to go."

We turn back to the wings. "I hope you break a leg tomorrow," Jacob says.

I snort. "I hope I don't. I'm already down one leg. I can't afford to wreck another one."

Jacob laughs.

It's the first laugh I've gotten tonight. As we walk offstage, I take it as a sign of good luck.

Twelve

"**H**ere you go, kiddo," Dad says as he slows to a stop in front of the theater at ten the next morning. Thank goodness Brooke and the twins aren't with us. When I met Mom in the hotel lobby a few minutes ago and she told me they were making their own way to the competition, I almost cried with relief.

I'm too nervous to see my sister right now.

My stomach flips as I stare out the window. I see a couple of news vans parked ahead of us: KPTV and KOIN 6. Reporters and camera operators too, standing by the theater entrance. I'm too nervous, period.

I can't believe TV news is here.

I can't believe *I'm* here.

I can't believe this is *really* happening.

"I'll find parking and let Mom and Grandpa walk you in." Dad glances back and winks at me. "Go get 'em, Paige. Show those guys just how great you are."

Mom opens the van door and gestures me out. The gray sky looks threatening, but it hasn't rained yet, and that's good news for my hair. In spite of all the expensive hair products Carly insisted I buy, and though I spent more than half an hour styling it this morning, I'm worried about frizzing up.

We walk toward the entrance. My heart begins to race. I'm about to face the biggest opportunity—and the biggest challenge—of my life. Making a crowd laugh. But I have to limp out onstage in front of them first.

Frizzing up is the least of my worries.

Grandpa slows in front of a heavily made-up blond holding a microphone. A bored-looking camera operator stands behind her. "This is my granddaughter. Paige Larsson." Grandpa drops his arm across my shoulders like he thinks I might run away or something. I look at Mom for support, but she's staring at the reporter and grinning like a fool. "She's competing in the video-comedy category. You'd better memorize her name. That's Larsson with two s's. You'll be hearing a lot about her in the coming years."

My cheeks burn. Where's that mega earth-quake when you need it? Right now, I'd give anything for the ground to open up and swallow me whole.

The woman gestures to the camera guy, who hoists his machine to his shoulders. She sticks the microphone under my nose. "How does it feel to be competing, Paige Larsson?"

I mumble something about it being a great opportunity and an honor to be shortlisted. I've barely finished speaking when someone else comes up, and the woman switches her attention to them.

Mom and Grandpa present their tickets at the entrance. I hold up my name tag for inspec-tion. The petite ticket checker, who's wearing eyelashes the length of my baby finger, smiles at me. "Go on in. And good luck."

Inside the door, a middle-aged usher with longish hair and kind brown eyes is waiting to take me backstage.·

"Why don't I walk down with you?" Mom straightens my vest, brushes something from my shoulder. I know there's nothing there. I spent over an hour primping. My jeans and vest are perfect. My makeup is perfect. If only *I* could be perfect. "Give you some support."

"Thanks, Mom, but only contestants are allowed backstage." I have no clue if that's true, but I don't want a mother escort.

"Okay then." Her blue eyes are full of emotion. "Remember, we love you, and we're proud of you no matter what happens up on that stage." She folds me into a hug. I breathe in her special mom smell: minty toothpaste, floral perfume and comfort.

The usher leads me through a metal door that goes backstage. "The first category is just wrapping up," he says as clapping breaks out in the theater. I hope Jacob makes it. He seems like a nice guy.

I follow the usher down the hall, past the turnoff to the stage and toward the dressing room. When I hear a burst of laughter, my heart starts to thrum. They'll stare at me as I walk into the room. I hate that.

They'll stare at you when you walk out onstage too.

Sometimes I wish I had a *Delete* button for my thoughts.

The usher stops by the open doorway. I freeze, suddenly conscious of my limp. "Here you are." He smiles before he turns away. "Good luck."

I stare at the crowd. There has to be at least sixty people in the room. Contestants wearing the flamboyant orange name tags, ushers in their burgundy jackets, a pile of organizers. But everybody is huddled around three TV monitors. Nobody is looking at me. I take a breath, walk in and stand awkwardly at the back of the group.

Jacob comes over. His face is flushed, and his hairline is damp with sweat. "Hey. Good morning."

"Good morning."

He's dressed casually in jeans, a white shirt and blue high-top runners. Aside from a few girls wearing leggings, and one guy wearing khakis, jeans seem to be the outfit of choice. My nervousness eases just a little. My walk may be messed up, but my clothes are perfect.

Jacob steers me over to a monitor. On the screen, I see the four judges sitting in the front row, iPads resting on their knees. Their heads are bent together. Raven Prest is sitting second from the end. My breath stalls. She's my all-time, hands-down favorite comedian. I can't believe she'll watch me perform today. It's like a dream come true. Except for the walking across the stage part.

"They're about to announce who made the first cut," Jacob tells me.

Twenty comedians start out in each category. Half will be eliminated after the first round this morning, and another half will be cut after this afternoon's round. Only five in each category will go on to tomorrow's final.

The judges straighten. The room goes quiet. I stare at the screen as one of the judges—British comedian Connor Hillis—looks into the camera and says, "I speak for all four of us when I say this was a difficult decision, and every contestant is to be congratulated for his or her efforts. Based on our criteria, here are the contestants in the straight stand-up comedy category who will compete in this afternoon's event."

Ten names flash onto the screen. There's a moment's pause and then comes a shout, followed by a burst of clapping. I barely have time to scan half the list before Jacob pulls me into a sweaty hug. "I made it." His voice trembles with emotion.

The next fifteen minutes are pandemonium as people are congratulated and consoled and the contestants in the first category trickle out of the room. I find a space against the wall and check my texts.

From Carly: **Good luck!!!!!!!!!!!!!!!!!**

From Hunter: **You're the funniest person I know. Remember that.**

From Mr. Roskinski: **Let the audience reaction guide you.**

The next half hour is a blur of instructions and final details. I listen as the organizers remind us that we'll be able to watch the event live on the monitor... that we'll be taken to the stage area ten minutes before our names will be called...that there will be a lunch for all contestants following our category.

Swallowing hard, I eye my competition. I recognize a guy from Idaho, one from Boston and another from Santa Fe. Girls from Tampa and Phoenix and Chicago. I've watched them all on YouTube. I've been awed by their talent.

Today they look as terrified as I feel. The thought doesn't offer much comfort.

As the competition in my category begins, I calmly watch the monitor along with everyone else. But by the time the fourth contestant starts into her routine, my panic reaches epic proportions.

These guys are good. Very, very good. Their material, their delivery, everything.

I don't measure up.

You're here. You're prepared. You need to give it your best shot.

I turn away from the monitor, lean back in my chair and mentally review my first routine. I changed it up last night when I realized Brooke would be in the audience. I needed to take out some of the stuff about her. So after meeting Carly and Hunter for dinner, I put in some fresh bits, smoothed out the transitions and practised until I was sure I'd memorized the changes. It's too bad, because Brooke is a great source of material. But as much as she pisses me off, there's no way I'll embarrass her in such a public way.

That's her style, not mine.

"Paige Larsson," a voice calls out.

My eyes fly open.

An usher with a belly the size of a small suitcase is standing in the doorway. "Paige Larsson," he repeats, glancing around the room. "You're up next."

I swallow the lump in my throat and stand.

108

Thirteen

I feel weirdly detached as I follow the guy down the hall. Like I'm floating above my body. I hear talking off in the distance, but it only vaguely registers. I see the girl from Chicago coming toward us, her face flushed, looking like she's going to cry.

I want to tell her it's okay, that she did her best, that whatever happens, happens. That there's not a thing we can do because the results are out of our control anyway.

Of course, I say nothing. I hold the words inside me instead, silently repeating them over and over like a mantra.

You've done your best. Whatever happens, happens. There's nothing you can do about it now.

I feel all floaty and Zen-like as I follow that usher. But when he stops beside the door marked *Stage*, my heart leaves the Zen zone for panic city.

OhGodohGodohGod. It's happening.

Holding a finger to his lips, he opens the door and motions me inside.

Like last night, the lights backstage are dim. But unlike last night, the place is crawling with crew. They move silently between the cables and under the scaffolding, an army of black T-shirts focused on one thing only: doing whatever they need to do to support the performer onstage.

We stop at the edge of the wings. I stare at the guy in the spotlight. Andrew somebody or other. From Boston. He's good, and he's getting lots of laughs. But his words don't register. I peer into the audience. It's dark. I can't see them. But I know they're there. Hundreds of people who will watch me walk across the stage. Who'll listen to my routine. Who will laugh. Or not.

Hundreds of people who can make or break me.

At least Hunter and Carly are here. They'll laugh. My parents and Grandpa will too. I'm suddenly grateful they've come.

It seems like only seconds later that Andrew is finished. There's a roar of white noise in my head as I hear the announcer say the next contestant is from Seattle. He mentions the name of my school and my YouTube channel. And then he says, "Please welcome Paige Larsson!"

I freeze.

The usher gives me a gentle shove. "Go!"

Knees knocking, I'm suddenly walking across the stage. My breath is coming so hard and fast I'm pretty sure it could power a small city. It takes me a century to reach that damned microphone. By the time I get there, I'm already sweating.

"You think that walk across the stage was slow..." My voice booms. I jerk back from the microphone. The spotlight hurts my eyes. "At least I didn't walk out here in stilettos. I might have killed myself. Or maimed my good leg."

There's a smattering of laughter. The relief I feel is almost palpable. I have the audience on side. Or part of it, at least. And that's the first thing any comedian needs to do.

"And what's up with stilettos anyway?" I need to slow down—I'm talking too fast. "Did you know there's a gym in New York that offers a stiletto workout?" There's another ripple of laughter. So far, so good. "Yeah. It's true. Like squats and lunges aren't painful enough without doing them while you're balancing on five-inch heels as skinny as needles?"

There's a holler from the left. "You go, sister!"

I start to laugh. My confidence gains a little more traction. "I know, right?" Even though I can't see faces, I make sure I look from left to right. I want people to feel like I'm talking directly to them. "I mean, working out in stilettos is guaranteed to give you skinnier thighs, except it's also a great way to break a leg or dislocate a shoulder." I pause, wait one beat. Two beats. "But at least you'll look hot when they load you into the ambulance."

The laughter is loud and long. There's clapping too. I can't stop grinning. I'm doing it. I'm really doing it!

"I don't get it," I say when the laughter fades. "But who am I to talk? I was born wrong. My feet won't let me do stilettos, and my brain won't let me do Sephora. Honestly, you need a degree in frivolous to shop there." The laughs keep coming, and before long I'm heading back to the dressing room, trembling with the rush of adrenaline and success.

I did okay. Better than okay, I decide as I sit in the corner of the dressing room under an auto-graphed picture of Prince. I did great. I scroll through congratulatory texts from Hunter, Carly and Mom. They all say so.

But was I great enough to make the next round?

Since only four people come after me, I don't have to wait long to find out. Soon the room falls silent as everyone sits and watches the judges on the monitor.

Please let me make the next round. Please.

The judges lift their heads. For the second time this morning, Connor Hillis congratulates everybody for taking part. "And here are the ten people in the video comedy category who will go on to this afternoon's round."

My heart slams against my chest as I stare at the screen. The letters are a mess of squiggles, and it takes me a second to skim down the list.

I'm there. Paige Larsson. Three-quarters of the way down.

I let out a breath I didn't know I was holding.

I'm going to round two.

* * *

Though Hunter and Carly urge me to join them for lunch, organizers bring in pizza, submarine sandwiches and bottles of soda, so I decide to eat backstage with the others. Our category is up first after lunch, and I don't want the distraction of leaving and then coming back.

With the first round successfully behind us, the mood in the room is upbeat. Over slices of Meat Lovers Supreme, I talk to Andrew, the guy from Boston who bleats like a sheep when he laughs, and the girl named Robyn who already has fourteen thousand YouTube followers. We exchange stories, admit to being nervous and try to one-up each other with one-liners about the city of Portland.

By the time I'm ushered down the hall to do my second routine, I'm in the zone. Feeling confident. Five of us will be chosen to go on to the final, and I'm pretty sure I'll be one of them. So this time when the announcer calls my name and I take that slow walk across the stage to the microphone, I'm practically relaxed.

Okay, maybe not, but my knees are hardly shaking and I'm hyperventilating only a little. Which is way better than the first time.

"You've heard of the slow-food movement," I say when I reach the microphone. I don't jump this time when my voice bounces back at me. I welcome the heat from the spotlight. The darkness where I know the audience sits. "Well, I'm the poster girl for the slow-move movement." A single titter from somewhere far back in the theater.

I stare down to where I know the judges are sitting. Funny isn't only about telling a joke—it's a way of connecting. And I need to connect with them. "I have a twisted perspective on life. It goes with my twisted leg."

Silence. My chest constricts. There's interested silence and bored silence. A trickle of sweat rolls down my back. What kind of silence is this? I'm not sure. "Which goes with my twisted hair."

I launch into my hair-product routine, but I'm talking too fast and not giving the audience time to respond, and the energy in the audience feels off. Or maybe it's me. "Honestly," I say as I wrap up the end of that bit, "my hair's better fed than I am."

I hear a few gentle chuckles, but it's not enough. I start to sweat. I don't have the audience. Too many of my jokes are falling flat. I go into my bit about my disability. "I was born wrong." I launch into my sleeping-on-the-job-in-utero routine, ending with a barb about sales clerks who think I'm deaf and dumb because I limp.

I get laughs, but they're uncomfortable, awkward laughs, and even the clapping seems less than enthusiastic. With my stomach in knots, I walk offstage and slowly make my way back down the hall.

I sucked.

In the dressing room, Andrew offers me a high five. "Good job," he says. The other contestants all avoid my gaze.

No wonder. I pretty much bombed.

Everybody blows it sometimes, I tell myself. Every comic, every actor, every dancer. They all fall flat once in a while. It's part of the job.

But why did I have to fall flat now?

In my pocket, my phone vibrates. Ignoring it, I sit in the corner and wait for the judges to rule. How will I face Hunter and Carly when I don't make the cut? How will I face Brooke? What will

I say to Mr. Roskinski? To my drama friends who are counting on me and that ten thousand dollars for the drama department?

"Here they go," someone says.

I look up. There's Connor Hillis again. My breath jams in my throat. I drop my head. I can't watch. I don't want to know.

After a minute, excited shouts break out. But it's not until Andrew taps me on the shoulder and says, "Congratulations," that I look up.

He points to the monitor.

I see my name. Paige Larrson. I'm last on the list.

But I made it. I'm going to the final round.

Fourteen

hat night, when Dad treats us all to dinner at a small, dimly lit Italian restaurant, everybody's full of congratulations and encouragement. Nobody seems to think my final routine sucked or seems concerned that I was the last finalist named. Even Mr. Roskinski brushed it off when I saw him afterward. He said I did well, though I still talked too fast.

"They weren't in any particular order." Carly twirls pesto linguine into an egg-shaped mound on her fork. "Don't even think about that."

Hunter, his mouth full of lasagna, nods. So do Mom and Dad. Brooke and the twins are too busy flirting with the dimpled waiter to comment. (I don't blame them. He looks totally like Liam Hemsworth.)

"All you need to think about is tomorrow," Grandpa says. Buttery bread crumbs dust his gray sweater. "You're going to win, Paige. I know you are."

"And don't worry about that second routine," Mom adds. She's been so busy praising me, she's hardly touched her veal parmesan. "It's not easy doing two routines back to back like that." She smiles. "You watch. Tomorrow will be easier."

I hope she's right. I go to bed that night with Mom's words on my mind, and I'm still thinking about them the next morning when I get up to shower and dress. I spend extra time on my hair and makeup. I even wear a red top with my jeans, hoping Carly's right and it'll energize me and the audience.

"You didn't invite anyone either?" Andrew asks when I walk into the dressing room just before eleven. We're allowed to invite friends or family to be backstage with us today. Judging by the number of people in the room, most contestants have. The place is packed, and the mood is loud and upbeat.

"No." We grab the last two chairs, at the far end of the room by the makeup stations.

"I'm too nervous to want anybody here," Andrew admits.

My stomach is twisted into a million knots. "Me too." I'll see people in the theater as we wait for the results. The winners in both categories will be announced at the same time. Thankfully, our category is second, so we won't have long to wait. Andrew and I sit quietly and watch the people around us until he's called to go on. He's up first.

"Good luck," I say. But as I watch him walk through the door, I feel small and petty and deceitful because a part of me doesn't mean it. There's only so much luck to go around, and I want it all.

When it's my turn to follow the usher down the hall, I'm so light-headed I'm almost dizzy. I force myself to stare at the weave on the back of his burgundy shirt, to think about everything Mr. Roskinski has taught me, everything I know. *Concentrate. Own the stage. Talk slowly. Use the silence. Engage the audience.*

Time seems to speed up. It feels like only seconds later that I'm in the wings watching Robyn finish her routine. And then the announcer calls my name.

My breath jams my throat. Ignoring it, I start to walk. Fear isn't allowed. Neither is panic or doubt or second thoughts.

I'm in this to win. I can't let people down.

"I would've come out here at a run," I say when I reach the microphone, "but I wanted to build suspense." I get a laugh. A good, solid one. Thank God.

My heart is so loud in my chest, I worry the microphone will pick up the sound. "It's kind of like when I took driving lessons last year and kept the instructor in suspense too." I realize I'm talking too fast, and I force myself to slow down. "We'd be coming up to a stop sign and he'd be telling me to brake, and it would take me a while, but I'd get to it eventually." Sweat trickles down my spine. Man, the lights seem hotter today. "A couple of times I even managed to do it before the middle of the intersection."

There's another round of laughter, and it lasts longer this time. Glancing over the audience, I say, "Trouble was, I like to speed. I figure if I can't walk fast, I may as well drive fast, right?"

A couple of hoots and a smattering of laughter. "Slow down, my instructor kept saying.

One day he told me I had a lead foot." I wait, let the silence build. "Thanks for clarifying that, I told him. I always wondered what was wrong."

And the theater erupts.

I laugh too. I'm doing well. I can feel it. I talk about driving alone for the first time and going to the supermarket. "They need to rename those self-checkout counters. You get in line to check yourself out, and seconds later a bell beeps and there's some kind of screwup and somebody comes to help, and then an item doesn't have a code, so another person comes to figure that out, only they need the manager because the item is on sale, so he comes to do a manual override, and pretty soon you have an entire team of people beside you." The laughter comes again, which is good because I'm talking too fast. "It's the super-market's new version of the express line."

I end with my bit about my name and how it means "servant" while my sister got the better deal because her name means she's always on the move and she doesn't have to answer to anybody but God. Before I know it, I'm walking off the stage, shaking but happy. I've left the audience laughing. I did the best I could.

I just hope my best was good enough.

Back in the theater, I quietly take my seat between Hunter and Carly. A couple of people give me a thumbs-up. Mr. Roskinski mouths, "Great job." I hardly hear a word of the last two performances. Instead, I'm reliving every word I said onstage, hearing every laugh all over again.

By the time the judges take the stage to announce the winners, I've bitten three nails.

Carly slaps my hand as I start on the fourth one. "Stop!"

Raven Prest steps forward to speak into the microphone. Blood pounds in my ears. "We've seen an incredible amount of talent this year, which has made the decision-making especially difficult." The oversized gold hoops in her ears shimmer under the bright lights. "And we'd like to offer our sincere congratulations to all the contestants for making it this far. But, unfortunately, there can only be one winner in each category." She pauses. "In the straight stand-up comedy category, the winner is Alexander Stein."

There's a shout about ten rows ahead. Not Jacob, I realize as I join in the clapping. Poor guy.

The clapping fades. "And now for the video comedy category," Raven Prest says.

My heart's hammering. I lean forward, grip the edge of my seat. *Please let me win. Please.*

"In that category, the winner is Robyn Paul."

The air disappears from my lungs. There's a shriek somewhere off to my right. I slump into my chair. Tears feather the back of my throat, a nasty mix of disappointment, shame and humiliation.

I lost. There'll be no agency representation. No trip to New York. No ten grand for me or the school. I catch Brooke's eye. She smirks and then turns to one of the twins. I almost cry. Around me, my friends and family offer their support.

Carly: "I don't get it. You're better than her."

Mom: "We think you're a winner."

Grandpa: "Those damned judges screwed up."

Hunter: "You'll win next year for sure."

I nod and smile and thank them. But it doesn't matter what they say. I gave it my best shot, and I lost. I let everybody down. And I let myself down too.

*   *   *

After a while I manage to sneak away to the bath-room. I hide in a stall and let the tears fall. People come and go. Toilets flush. Hands get washed. Just about everybody talks about the contest. Someone even mentions my name. She says I was pretty good.

I hold that comment close. I pretend I'm my own best friend. I tell myself I was brave to go out there in the first place, especially when I was so freaking scared. I remind myself that I'm not meant to be onstage anyway. YouTube is where it's at. YouTube is where I belong.

When I'm finished crying and the bathroom is quiet, I open the door and come out.

Brooke is leaning against the vanity. Bottle rockets go off in my chest. She watches me walk to the sink. "I told Mom I'd come and see if you're okay." Her voice is almost gentle.

She cares. The tears are back, crowding the back of my throat. I retrieve a paper towel and look at us in the mirror. She's tall blond perfection, and I'm short red frizz. But in spite of everything, we are sisters. And finally I'm looking at the sister I remember from when I was really little. "Thanks." I swallow my tears and moisten the paper towel under the tap. "I'm okay."

She crosses her arms. "Mostly I wanted to tell you you're not funny." Her voice hardens. "You're an embarrassment. And now you're a loser. How do you think that makes me look?"

"Huh?"

"You heard me."

Heat hits the back of my neck. With it comes that black pit of self-hate. The one that started in elementary school when Brooke laughed with the mean boys. I blot my swollen eyes. "This isn't about you."

Her lips thin. "Yeah, it is. You're my sister. You limp. And for months you've been making an ass of yourself trying to get people to laugh."

I don't try. I do it.

"People talk," she continues. "And I hate it."

The heat climbs into my cheeks. I cover them with the paper towel. I put everything I had into this contest. I took a huge risk putting myself out there. And all Brooke can think about is herself? Unbelievable. My shame hardens to anger.

"I'm sorry you feel that way." I manage, just barely, to keep my voice steady.

"It's time you gave this whole comedy thing up."

No way. For a minute when I lost—okay, maybe for two minutes—I thought about it. For sure I wanted to hide under a rock somewhere. But give up? Not gonna happen. "I'm not stopping. Comedy is a part of me. Like my limp is." It's the first time I've said that to my sister. It actually feels good.

Brooke's eyes, flat with anger, meet mine in the mirror. That's when I realize today's loss doesn't matter. Even if I'd won, Brooke would be mad. I'm a disappointment to her. And I always will be.

"You are such a freak," she says.

I'm totally sick of that word. But this time my anger is mixed with sadness. I can't believe how bitter and hateful Brooke is. It must suck to carry all that negativity around. To be her. "We all have our freakish bits." I drop my soiled paper towel into the wastebasket.

She looks confused.

"At least mine are on the outside," I tell her as I head for the exit. "It's better than having them on the inside like you."

And I slam the door behind me.

Fifteen

"**D**on't be so hard on yourself," Carly says a couple of hours later as we walk down the hall to the theater's administration offices. Contestants have to sign release papers to allow the ITCF to use photographs or footage for future promotions. I was so upset after the exchange with Brooke, I almost forgot. "The fact that you made the finals is huge."

"I guess, but I'm never doing stand-up again." I'll give Brooke that much.

"Never say never," Carly says.

I glare at her. "Never."

She rolls her eyes.

"I appreciate you and Hunter nominating me, but walking across that stage"—*limping across that stage*—"was torture." And Brooke calling me an embarrassment later was torture too.

She rolls her eyes. "Oh my god, don't be such a drama queen."

We stop beside the door to the administration office. Inside, two contestants from the other category are standing at a long counter, signing papers. I don't know them, and I'm glad. I don't want to talk to anybody. I don't even want to take the bus back home. I'm driving back with Mom and Dad instead. "Wait here," I tell Carly. "I'll just be a minute."

At the counter, a plump, middle-aged woman with her hair pulled into a tight bun is flipping through a stack of beige envelopes. "Your name?" She doesn't even look at me.

"Paige Larsson."

Her fingers stop moving. Her head rises. There's a curious look in her eyes. "One minute, please." She disappears into the back. I glance at Carly, but she's on her phone and not paying any attention.

"Paige Larsson."

The voice is vaguely familiar, but I don't realize who's speaking until I turn back and see the woman standing there. My breath catches. I stare at her. "Raven Prest?"

Her laugh is low and husky. "The one and only." She gestures behind her. "Come on back. I'd like to talk to you for a minute."

My knees feel all rubbery as she leads me around the counter and down a hall. Raven Prest wants to talk *to me?* Stunned, I follow her into a small boardroom. Half a dozen black padded chairs frame an oval table.

"Have a seat."

I take the chair beside her. I'm close enough that I could touch her. The thought leaves me speechless. I want to tell her I love her work, that I'm a huge fan. That I know I'm lousy at stand-up, that it was my friends who nominated me. But all I can do is stare and think stupid, dumb thoughts like, She has a really, really long neck, and, God, that diamond she's wearing on her finger is practically the size of a chicken nugget.

"I've seen your YouTube videos." She crosses one booted leg over the other. "You're good. You have great timing and a funny way of looking at the world."

There's a whooshing sound in my head. Raven Prest thinks I'm *good*? "Thanks." My voice comes out in a stammer. I sound like a fool.

"But you almost didn't make the final round."

Am I dreaming? First she says I'm good, and then she says I almost didn't make the final. "I didn't?"

"No. Your second routine almost got you disqualified."

I knew it was bad. "I had trouble with it."

She nods. "That was obvious. But instead of reaching for something everybody could relate to, you fell back on your disability. I suspect that's your default place to go, making fun of yourself?"

She's right. Hunter hated it too. I nod.

"Well, if you're going to get anywhere in the world of comedy, you need to focus on a broader picture. It's one thing to comment on your disability like you did in your driving routine, but don't make it the focus. The world doesn't need more 'poor me' stuff."

Poor me? Is that what she thinks I'm about? That I feel sorry for myself? Everything I want to say crowds into my throat. I've been trying to get my limp front and center, trying to put it out there before anybody else could. "I've been trying to avoid pity," I finally manage to say.

She stares at me for a minute. Her dark eyes look almost black against the crisp white of her button-down shirt. "Fair enough. But by being afraid that people will laugh at you instead of with you, you've sold yourself out. You're in danger of becoming the comedian with the limp instead of Paige Larsson, the comedian."

The truth hits me like a slap. She's right. Heat floods my face.

"Look, you have tremendous potential. With a little guidance, you could go places. If you're truly serious about comedy and are willing to work hard, I'll help you," Raven says. "I'll do Skype sessions with you once a month, and we'll go over your material."

I can't believe what I'm hearing. "Seriously? You'd help me with my video routines?"

"No." Raven shakes her head. "I'd help you with your *comedy* routines. All of them. Stand-up and improv and video comedy."

My stomach sinks. It's the opportunity of a lifetime. The other contestants would kill to be in my shoes. But there's no way I'll put myself through that again. "I can't do stand-up. Or improv."

"You think you can't. I think you're afraid."

The heat in my face races down my neck. Maybe I am a little.

"I know what it's like. When I went from YouTube to stand-up, I had such bad stage fright I'd puke before I went onstage. Every single time." She laughs. "It was my very own lose-weight-without-trying program."

My eyes widen. "I can't believe it." She looks so natural onstage.

"Believe it. It got so bad I almost gave up." She looks at her watch. She needs to be somewhere, I can tell. "If you're a true comedian, you need to master every aspect of comedy, even the stuff that scares you." She gives me a half smile. "You have to be prepared to step out there."

I am a true comedian. At least, I want to be. I look down at my hands. A pressure in my chest makes it hard to breathe. But if I step out, I have to be prepared to fall down. Maybe that's what separates the true comedians from the wannabes. Being prepared to bomb. My heart crowds into my throat. Do I have the guts to risk bombing again?

I look back up, take a deep breath. If I really want this, I have no choice. "Okay." I'm giddy with excitement and fear and gratitude. "I'll do it." I blink back tears. "Thank you."

"You're welcome. I'm looking forward to working with you." She stands. "With luck, you'll be back on that stage next year."

* * *

"So what's your story today, Larsson?" Ms. Vastag asks when she stops beside my library cubicle at school Monday afternoon. I spot Hunter walking through the door. Brooke, who's sitting with one of the twins, waves at him. "Why aren't you in gym?"

"I have a bad cold." It's true. I stayed home this morning, and if I didn't have a math quiz next block, I'd still be under a blanket on the couch.

She frowns. "And I have hemorrhoids. Big deal."

I start to laugh.

"You think that's funny?" But her words have no punch, and there's a glint of amusement in her eyes.

"Not really." But I do. With her delivery, Ms. Vastag could be onstage. Hunter walks by and wiggles his eyebrows at me. I give him a little wave.

Ms. Vastag watches him pull out a chair at a nearby table before slouching against the cubicle and looking back down at me. "I heard about the competition." She looks especially colorful today with her rainbow-striped socks and purple Birkenstocks. "I'm sorry you lost. Word is you killed it onstage though."

"Yeah, well, I didn't kill it enough to win." I still feel rotten about letting people down. Mr. Roskinski's been great about it, and so have my friends, but that doesn't take away my disappointment.

"Like I said last week, life's a poker hand. There's always another game coming. As long as you pick up the cards and deal yourself in."

"I guess." Maybe I'll get shortlisted for the ITCF next year. If I don't let fear or doubt or Brooke's mean comments get to me. I still hope one day we'll be close again. That she'll stop resenting me and grow up. But it may not happen for a long time, if ever. Life doesn't come with a guarantee.

Ms. Vastag bends down. She's so close I can see the coffee stains on her front teeth. "I see Brooke's trying to move in on your territory."

I look at Brooke. She's practically jumping out of her chair trying to get Hunter's attention. I look back at Ms. Vastag. *Territory*? Did I hear her right? Has the cold plugged my ears?

"Hunter MacRae," she whispers.

I'm stunned. Ms. Vastag isn't like any other teacher in the school, but this is getting personal, even for her. "He's not my territory. He doesn't belong to me."

She rolls her eyes. "Maybe not, but the guy's been following you around like a homeless puppy for the last six months. You need to put him out of his misery and tell him how you feel."

Oh jeez. Is it that obvious? Does everybody know? I look at Brooke again. Does she? Is that why she's been throwing herself at Hunter lately?

Ms. Vastag follows my gaze. "Brooke wants what you have," she says. "She's threatened because you're funny and she's not."

Brooke's just jealous. I flash on Hunter's words. Maybe he's right about that too.

"Forget your sister." She inclines her head ever so slightly toward Hunter. "Well? Are you going to just sit there?"

What? Ms. Vastag is telling me to go talk to Hunter? No way. The cold *is* messing with my head.

She gives me a pointed look. "Don't be a wuss, Larsson. Remember that other thing I told you? We've all got something." She stops, presumably waiting for me to answer. When I don't, she smiles and says, "Just don't let your something get in the way of having a life."

It's the smile that gets me. That's only the second time Ms. Vastag has smiled since grade eight. It has to be a sign. I look at Brooke. I look at Hunter. Then I push my chair back and stand.

It's time to get in the game.

Acknowledgments

Thanks to Sarah Harvey, who got the ball rolling, to Barry for insisting comedy isn't all that scary, and to Zach for insightful comments along the way.

LAURA LANGSTON is the award-winning author of nineteen books for children and young adults, including *Hot New Thing* in the Orca Limelights series. When she's not writing, reading or walking her Shetland sheepdogs, Laura can usually be found spying on people in the grocery store or twisting herself into a pretzel in yoga class. For more information, visit www.lauralangston.com.

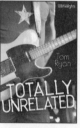